ACCLAIM FOR RICHARD RUSSO'S

The Whore's Child

Winner of the *Southern Review*'s Short Fiction Award

"These beautifully crafted stories, made more appealing by their rueful humor, are the work of a writer at the top of his game."
—*New York Post*

"Russo is a master of the small moment as nuclear explosion, the life-changing turn of the screw. His writing is unornate, but as authoritative (and cool) as marble. . . . *The Whore's Child* is . . . powerful and moving."
—*The Atlanta Journal-Constitution*

"The vigorous comic voice that has always been Russo's is a great leavening force here. . . . These stories are something to be grateful for."
—*Newsday*

"*The Whore's Child* pulsate[s] with real life."
—*The New Leader*

RICHARD RUSSO

The Whore's Child

Richard Russo lives with his wife in Camden, Maine, and in Boston. In 2002 he was awarded the Pulitzer Prize for *Empire Falls*.

He is available for lectures and readings. For information regarding his availability, please visit www.knopfspeakersbureau.com or call 212-572-2013.

BOOKS BY RICHARD RUSSO

Mohawk

The Risk Pool

Nobody's Fool

Straight Man

The Whore's Child

Empire Falls

Bridge of Sighs

That Old Cape Magic

The Whore's Child

The Whore's Child

AND OTHER STORIES

RICHARD RUSSO

Vintage Contemporaries
Vintage Books
A Division of Random House, Inc.
New York

FIRST VINTAGE CONTEMPORARIES EDITION, JULY 2003

"The Whore's Child" was originally published in *Harper's*. "Monhegan
Light" was originally published in *Esquire*. "The Farther You Go"
was originally published in *Shenandoah*. "Joy Ride" was originally
published in *Meridian*. "Poison" was originally published in *Kiosk*.
"Buoyancy" was originally published in *High Infidelity*, ed. John
McNally (William Morrow, 1997).

The Library of Congress has cataloged the Knopf edition as follows:
Russo, Richard, [date]
The whore's child and other stories / Richard Russo.
p. cm.
ISBN 0-375-41168-2 (hc : alk. paper)
I. Title.
PS3568.U812 W48 2002
813'.54—dc21   2002019023

Vintage ISBN: 0375-72601-2

Book design by Virginia Tan

www.vintagebooks.com

Printed in the United States of America
10 9 8 7 6

For Jenny Boylan

Contents

Acknowledgments

Much gratitude to Gary Fisketjon, my editor and friend at Knopf, as well as to the editors of the publications these stories originally appeared in. Every one of my books has been made better thanks to the smart and loving attention bestowed upon them by Nat Sobel and Judith Weber. And always, always Barbara.

The Whore's Child

The Whore's Child

Sister Ursula belonged to an all but extinct order of
Belgian nuns who conducted what little spiritual business
remained to them in a decrepit old house purchased by
the diocese seemingly because it was unlikely to outlast
them. Since it was on Forest Avenue, a block from our
house, I'd seen Sister Ursula many times before the night
she turned up in class, but we never had spoken. She
drove a rusted-out station wagon that was always crowded
with elderly nuns who needed assistance getting in and
out. Though St. Francis Church was only a few blocks
away, that was too far to walk for any of them except
Sister Ursula, her gait awkward but relentless. "You
should go over there and introduce yourself someday,"
Gail, my wife, suggested more than once. "Those old
women have been left all alone." Her suspicion was later
confirmed by Sister Ursula herself. "They are waiting for
us to die," she confessed. "Impatient of how we clutch to
our miserable existences."

"I'm sure you don't mean that," I said, an observation that was to become my mantra with her, and she, in turn, seemed to enjoy hearing me say it.

She appeared in class that first night and settled herself at the very center of the seminar despite the fact that her name did not appear on my computer printout. Fiction writing classes are popular and invariably over-subscribed at most universities, and never more so than when the writer teaching it has recently published a book, as I had done the past spring. Publishing the kind of book that's displayed in strip-mall bookstores bestows a celebrity on academic writers and separates them from their scholar colleagues, whose books resemble the sort of dubious specialty items found only in boutiques and health food stores. I'd gotten quite a lot of press on my recent book, my first in over a decade, and my fleeting celebrity might have explained Sister Ursula's presence in my classroom the first chilly evening of the fall semes-ter, though she gave no indication of this, or that she rec-ognized me as her neighbor.

No, Sister Ursula seemed innocent not only of me but also of all department and university protocol. When informed that students petition to take the advanced fic-tion writing class by means of a manuscript submission the previous term, and that its prerequisites were begin-ning and intermediate courses, Sister Ursula disputed neither the existence nor the wisdom of these procedures. Nor did she gather her things and leave, which left me in an odd position. Normally it's my policy not to allow unregistered students to remain in class, because doing so encourages their mistaken belief that they can wheedle, cajole or flatter their way in. In the past I'd shown even football players the door without the slightest courtesy or ceremony, but this was a different challenge entirely. Sister Ursula herself was nearly as big as a linebacker, yet more persuasive than this was her body language, which suggested that once settled, she was not used to moving. And since she was clearly settled, I let her stay.

After class, however, I did explain why it would be highly unprofessional of me to allow her to remain in the advanced fiction workshop. After all, she freely admitted she'd never attempted to write a story before, which, I explained, put her at an extreme disadvantage. My mistake was in not leaving the matter there. Instead I went on. "This is a storytelling class, Sister. We're all liars here. The whole purpose of our enterprise is to become skilled in making things up, of substituting our own truth for *the* truth. In this class we actually prefer a well-told lie," I concluded, certain that this would dissuade her.

She patted my hand, as you might the hand of a child. "Never you mind," she then assured me, adjusting her wimple for the journey home. "My whole life has been a lie."

"I'm sure you don't mean that," I told her.

In the convent, Sister Ursula's first submission began, *I was known as the whore's child.*

Nice opening, I wrote in the margin, as if to imply that

her choice had been a purely artistic one. It wasn't, of course. She was simply starting with what was for her the beginning of her torment. She was writing—and would continue to write—a memoir. By mid-semester I would give up asking her to invent things.

The first installment weighed in at a robust twenty-five pages, which detailed the suffering of a young girl taken to live in a Belgian convent school where the treatment of the children was determined by the social and financial status of the parents who had abandoned them there. As a charity case and the daughter of a prostitute, young Sister Ursula (for there could be no doubt that she *was* the first-person narrator) found herself at the very bottom of the ecclesiastical food chain. What little wealth she possessed—some pens and paper her father had purchased for her the day before they left the city, along with a pretty new dress—was taken from her, and she was informed that henceforth she would have no use for such pitiful possessions. Her needs—food, a uniform and a single pair of shoes—would be provided for her, though she would doubtless prove unworthy to receive them. The shoes she was given were two sizes too small, an accident, Sister Ursula imagined, until she asked if she might exchange them for the shoes of a younger girl that were two sizes too large, only to be scorned for her impertinence. So before long she developed the tortured gait of a cripple, which was much imitated by the other children, who immediately perceived in her a suitable object for their cruelest derision.

The mockery of her classmates was something Sister

Ursula quickly accommodated, by shunning their companionship. In time she grew accustomed to being referred to as "the whore's child," and she hoped that the children would eventually tire of calling her this if she could manage to conceal how deeply it wounded her. During periods of recreation in the convent courtyard she perfected the art of becoming invisible, avoiding all games and contests when, she knew, even those on her own team would turn on her. What she was not prepared for was the cruelty she suffered at the hands of the nuns, who seemed to derive nearly as much satisfaction from tormenting her as their charges—beginning with her request to exchange shoes. She had not merely been told that this was not permitted, but was given a horrible explanation as to why this was so. The chafing of the too small shoes had caused her heels to bleed into her coarse white socks and then into the shoes themselves. Only a wicked child, Sister Veronique explained, would foul the shoes she'd been given with her blood, then beg to exchange them for the shoes of an innocent child. Did she think it fair, the old nun wondered out loud, that another child, one who had not only a virtuous mother but also a father, be asked to wear the polluted shoes of a whore's child?

Worse than the sting of the old nun's suggestion that anything Sister Ursula touched immediately became contaminated was the inference that trailed in the wake of her other remark. The innocent girl had not only a virtuous mother—Sister Ursula knew what this meant—*but also a father,* which seemed to imply that she herself didn't have one. Of course she knew that she did have a father, a tall, handsome father who had promised to rescue her from this place as soon as he could find work. Indeed, it was her father who had brought her to the convent, who had assured Mother Superior that she was a good girl and not at all wicked. How then had Sister Veronique concluded that she had no father? The young girl tried to reason it through but became confused. She knew from experience that evil, by its very nature, counted for more in the world than good. And she understood that her mother's being a prostitute made her "the whore's child," that her mother's wickedness diminished her father's value, but did it negate his very existence? How could such a thing be? She dared not ask, and so the old nun's remark burrowed even deeper, intensifying a misery that already bordered on despair.

Sister Ursula's first installment ended here, and her fellow students approached the discussion of it as one would an alien spacecraft. Several had attended Catholic schools where they'd been tutored by nuns, and they weren't sure, despite my encouragement, that they were allowed to be critical of this one. The material itself was foreign to them; they'd never encountered anything like it in the workshop. On the plus side, Sister Ursula's story had a character in it, and the character was placed in a dire situation, and those were good things for stories to do. On the other hand, the old nun's idiom was imperfect, her style stiff and old-fashioned, and the story seemed to be moving forward without exactly getting anywhere. It reminded them of stories they'd heard other elderly people tell, tales that even the tellers eventually managed to forget the point of, narratives that would gradually peter out with the weak insistence that all these events really did happen. "It's a victim story," one student recognized. "The character is being acted on by outside forces, but she has no choices, which means there can be no consequences to anything she does. If she doesn't participate in her own destiny, where's the story?"

Not having taken the beginning and intermediate courses, Sister Ursula was much enlightened by these unanticipated critiques, and she took feverish notes on everything that was said. "I liked it, though," added the student who'd identified it as a victim story. "It's different." By which he seemed to mean that Sister Ursula herself was different.

The old nun stopped by my office the day after, and it was clear she was still mulling the workshop over. "To be so much . . . a victim," she said, searching for the right words, "it is not good?"

"No," I smiled. Not in stories, not in life, I was about to add, until I remembered that Sister Ursula still wasn't making this distinction, and my doing so would probably confuse her further. "But maybe in the next installment?" I suggested.

She looked at me hopefully.

"Maybe your character will have some choices of her own as your story continues?" I prodded.

Sister Ursula considered this possibility for a long time, and I could tell by looking at her that the past wasn't nearly as flexible as she might have wished.

She was about to leave when she noticed the photograph of my daughter that I keep on my desk. "Your little girl," she said, "is a great beauty?"

"Yes," I said, indicating that it was okay to pick up the photo if she wanted to.

"Sometimes I see her when I am driving by," she explained. When I didn't say anything, she added, "Sometimes I don't see her anymore?"

"She and her mother are gone now," I explained, the sentence feeling syntactically strange, as if English were my second language, too. "They're living in another state."

Sister Ursula nodded uncertainly, as if deliberating whether "state" meant a condition or a place, then said, "She will return to this state?"

It was my turn to nod. "I hope so, Sister."

And so I became a Catholic, began the second installment of Sister Ursula's story, and again I scribbled *nice opening* in the left margin before hunkering down. I'd had students like Sister Ursula before, and they'd inspired the strictly enforced twenty-five page limit in all my workshops. I noted that for this second submission she had narrowed her margins, fiddled with the font, wedging the letters closer together. The spacing didn't look quite double, maybe 1.7. Venial sins.

Having had no religious training prior to entering the convent, Sister Ursula was for some time unable to recite prayers with the other children, further evidence, if any were needed, of the moral depravity inherent to being the offspring of a whore. She discovered it was not an easy task, learning prayers to the cadence of public ridicule, but learn them she did, and though the rote recitation was, in the beginning, a torment, it eventually became a comfort. Most of the prayers she fought to memorize were adamant about the existence of a God who, at least in the person of the crucified Christ, was infinitely more loving and understanding and forgiving than the women He'd led to the altar as His brides.

To be loved and understood and forgiven seemed to Sister Ursula the ultimate indulgence, and thus she became a denizen of the convent chapel, retreating there at every opportunity from the taunts and jeers of the other children and the constant crowlike reprimands of the nuns. She liked the smell of the place—damp and cool and clean—especially when she had it to herself, when it wasn't filled with the bodies of stale old nuns and sweaty children. Often she could hide in the chapel for an hour or more before one of the side doors would finally creak open, momentarily flooding the floor with bright light. Then the long dark shadow of a nun would fall across Sister Ursula where she knelt in prayer at the foot of the cross, and she would have no choice but to rise and be led back to her torment, often by a twisted ear.

In addition to the authorized prayers she'd memorized, Sister Ursula composed others of her own. She prayed that Sister Veronique, who had suggested that she had no father and who worked in the convent stable, might be kicked in the head by a horse and paralyzed for life. She prayed that Sister Joseph, who used her command of the kitchen to ensure that charity children were given the poorest food in the smallest quantities, might one day slip and fall into one of her boiling vats. Required herself to spend most holidays at the convent, Sister Ursula prayed that the children who were allowed to go home might perish in railway accidents. Sometimes, in an economical mood, she prayed that the convent might burn to the ground, and the air fill with black ash. She saw nothing wrong with offering such prayers, particularly since none of them, no matter how urgent, were ever answered. She felt a gentle trust in the Jesus of the Cross who hung above the main altar of the convent chapel. He seemed to know everything that was in her heart and to understand that nothing dwelt there that wasn't absolutely necessary to her survival. He would not begrudge her these prayers.

In truth, Jesus on the cross reminded Sister Ursula of her father who she knew had never wanted to see her packed off to the convent, and who missed her every day, just as she missed him. Like Jesus, her father was slender and handsome and sad; and unable to find work and married to a woman who was his shame. He was, like Jesus, stuck where he was. Yet if the prayers she had struggled to memorize were true, there was hope. Had not Jesus shed His crown of thorns, stepped down from the cross to become the light and salvation of the world, raising up with Him the lowly and the true of heart? Sister Ursula, when she wasn't praying that a horse kick Sister Veronique in the head, fervently prayed that her father might one day be free. The first thing he would do, she felt certain, was come for her, and so every time the chapel's side door opened, she turned toward the harsh light with a mixture of hope and fear, and though it was always a nun whose dark silhouette filled the doorway, she held tenaciously to the belief that soon it would be her father standing there.

One Christmas season—was it her third year at the convent school?—Sister Ursula was summoned to the chamber of Mother Superior, who told her to ready herself for a journey. This was a full week before any of the other students would be permitted to leave for the Christmas holiday, and Sister Ursula was instructed to tell no one of her impending departure. Indeed, Mother Superior seemed flustered, and this gave Sister Ursula heart. During her years of secret, vengeful prayer she'd indulged many fantasies of dramatic liberation, and often imagined her father's arrival on horseback, his angry pounding at the main gate, his purposeful stride through the courtyard and into the chapel. Perhaps Mother Superior's anxiety stemmed from the fact that her father was already on his way to effect just such a rescue.

At the appointed hour, Sister Ursula waited, as instructed, by the main gate, beyond which no men save priests were permitted entry, and awaited her father's arrival. She hoped he would come by a coach or carriage that then would convey them to the village train station, but if necessary she was more than happy to make the journey on foot, so long as she and her father were together. She had better shoes now, though she still hobbled like a cripple. And so when a carriage came into view in the dusty road beyond the iron gate, her heart leapt up—until she recognized it as the one belonging to the convent. Inside sat not her father but Sister Veronique, who had not been kicked in the head by a horse despite three years' worth of Sister Ursula's dogged prayers. When the carriage drew to a halt, Sister Ursula understood that her hopes had been led astray by her need and that she was to be banished from the convent, not rescued from it. She did not fear a worse existence than her present one, because a worse existence was not within her powers of imagination. Rather, what frightened her was the possibility that if she was taken from the convent school, her father no longer would know where to find her when the time came. This terrible fear she kept to herself. She and Sister Veronique did not speak a word on the long journey to the city.

Late that evening they arrived at a hospital and were taken to the charity ward, only to learn that Sister Ursula's mother had expired just after they had left the convent that morning. A nun dressed all in white informed Sister Veronique that it would be far better for the child not to see the deceased, and a look passed between them. All that was left by way of a keepsake was a brittle, curling, scallop-edged photograph, which the white nun gave to Sister Ursula, who had offered no reaction to the news that her mother was dead. Since arriving at the hospital, Sister Ursula had lapsed into a state of paralytic fear that it was her father who had fallen ill there. Instead, it seemed at least one of her prayers had been answered: her father was free.

But where was he? When she summoned the courage to ask, the two nuns exchanged another glance, in which it was plain that the white nun shared Sister Veronique's belief that she had no father, and Sister Ursula saw, too, that it would be useless for her, a child, to try to convince the white nun otherwise. Her fury supported her during their train ride, but then, when the convent came into view from the carriage, Sister Ursula broke down and began to sob. To her surprise, if not comfort, Sister Veronique placed a rough, callused hand on her shoulder and said softly, "Never mind, child. You will become one of us now." In response Sister Ursula slid as far away from the old nun as she could and sobbed even harder, knowing it must be true.

"Are we ever going to meet the father?" one student wanted to know. "I mean, she yearns for him, and he gets compared to Christ, but we never see him directly. We're, like, *told* how to feel about him. If he doesn't ever show up, I'm going to feel cheated."

Sister Ursula dutifully noted this criticism, but you had only to look at the old woman to know that the father was not going to show up. Anybody who felt cheated by this could just join the club.

The day after Sister Ursula's second workshop, my doorbell rang at seven-thirty in the morning. I struggled out of bed, put on a robe and went to the door. Sister Ursula stood on the porch, clearly agitated. The forlorn station wagon idled at the curb with its full cargo of curious, myopic nuns, returning, I guessed, from morning Mass. The yard was strewn with dry, unraked November leaves, several of which had attached themselves to the bottom of Sister Ursula's flowing habit.

"Must he be in the story? Must he return?" Sister Ursula wanted to know. As badly as she had wanted her father to appear in life, she needed, for some reason, to exclude him from the narrative version.

"He's already *in* the story," I pointed out, cinching my robe tightly at the waist.

"But I never saw him after she died. This is what my story is about."

"How about a flashback?" I suggested. "You mentioned there was one Christmas holiday . . ."

But she was no longer listening. Her eyes, slate gray, had gone hard. "She died of syphilis."

I nodded, feeling something harden in me too. Behind me I heard the bathroom door open and close, and I thought I saw Sister Ursula's gaze flicker for an instant. She might have caught a glimpse of Jane, the woman I was involved with, and I found myself hoping she had.

"My father's heart was broken."

"How do you know that, if you never saw him again?"

"He loved her," she explained. "She was his ruin."

It was my hatred that drew me deeper into the Church, began Sister Ursula's third installment, the words cramped even more tightly on exactly twenty-five pages, and this elicited my now standard comment in the margin. As a writer of opening sentences, Sister Ursula was without peer among my students.

In the months following her mother's death, an explanation had occurred to Sister Ursula. Her father, most likely, had booked passage to America to search for work. Such journeys, she knew, were fraught with unimaginable peril, and perhaps he now lay at the bottom of the ocean. So it was that she gradually came to accept the inevitability of Sister Veronique's cruel prophecy. She would become one of those whom she detested. Ironically, this fate was hastened by the prophet's untimely death when she was kicked by a horse, not in the head as Sister Ursula had prayed, but in the chest, causing severe internal hemorrhaging and creating an opening in the stable. During her long sojourn at the convent, Sister Ursula had learned to prefer the company of animals to that of humans, and so at the age of sixteen, already a large, full woman like her mother, she became herself a bride of Christ.

Sister Ursula's chronicle of the years following her vows, largely a description of her duties in the stable, featured several brief recollections of the single week she'd spent at home in the city during the Christmas holiday of that first year she entered the convent school. During that holiday she'd seen very little of her mother—a relief, since Sister Ursula dreaded the heat of her mother's embrace and the cloying stench of her whore's perfume. Rather, her beloved father took her with him on his rounds, placing her on a convenient bench outside the dark buildings he entered, telling her how long he would be, how high a number she would have to count to before he would return. Only a few times did she have to count higher. "Did you find work, Father?" she asked each time he reappeared. It seemed to Sister Ursula that in buildings as large and dark as the ones he entered, with so many other men entering and exiting, there should have been work in one of them, but there was none. Still, that they were together was joy enough. Her father took her to the wharf to see the boats, to a small carnival where a man her father knew let her ride a pony for free and finally to a bitter cold picnic in the country where they ate warm bread and cheese. At the end of each of these excursions her father promised again that she would not have to remain much longer in the convent school, that another Christmas would find them together.

The installment ended with Sister Ursula taking her final vows in the same chapel that for years had been her refuge from the taunts of children for whom she would always be the whore's child. There, at the very altar of God, Sister Ursula, like a reluctant bride at an arranged marriage, indulged her fantasy of rescue right up to the last moment. When asked to proclaim her irrevocable devotion to God and the one true Church, she paused and turned toward the side door of the chapel, the one she'd always imagined her father would throw open, and willed her father's shadow to emerge from the blinding light and scatter these useless women and hateful children before him.

But the door remained shut, the chapel dark except for the flickering of a hundred candles, and so Sister Ursula became a bride.

"Isn't there a lot of misogyny in this story?" observed a male student who I happened to know was taking a course with the English department's sole radical feminist, and was therefore alert to all of misogyny's insidious manifestations. By stating this opinion in the form of a question, perhaps he was indicating that the distrust and even hatred of women evident in Sister Ursula's memoir might be okay in this instance because the author was, sort of, a woman.

At any rate, he was right to be cautious. What would you expect, a chorus of his female classmates sang out.

The whole thing takes place in a girls' school. There were only two men in the story and one was Jesus, so the statistical sample was bound to be skewed. No, read correctly, Sister Ursula was clearly a feminist.

"I *would* like to see more of the mother, though," one young woman conceded. "It was a major cop-out for her to die before they could get to the hospital."

"You wanted a deathbed scene?" said another. "Wouldn't that be sort of melodramatic?"

Here the discussion faltered. Melodrama was a bad thing, almost as bad as misogyny.

"Why was the daughter sent for?" wondered someone else. "If the mother didn't love her, why send for her?"

"Maybe the father sent for her?"

"Then why wasn't he there himself?"

"I know I was the one," interrupted another, "who wanted to see more of the father after the last submission, but now I think I was wrong. All that stuff with her father over the Christmas holiday? It was like we kept hearing what we already knew. And *then* he's not there at the hospital when the mother dies. I'm confused." He turned to me. "Aren't you?"

"Maybe somebody in the hospital contacted the convent," another student suggested, letting me off the hook.

"For a dying prostitute in a charity ward? How would they even know where the daughter was unless the mother told them?"

Everyone now turned to Sister Ursula, who under this barrage of questions seemed to have slipped into a trance.

"I don't care," said another student, one of the loners in the back of the room. "I *like* this story. It feels real."

· · ·

The fourth and final installment of Sister Ursula's story was only six and a half pages long with regular margins, normal fonts and standard double-spacing.

My life as a nun has been one of terrible hatred and bitterness, it began. I considered writing, *You don't mean that,* in the margin, but refrained. Sister Ursula always meant what she said. It was now late November, and she hadn't veered a centimeter from literal truth since Labor Day. These last, perfunctory pages summarized her remaining years in the convent until the school was partially destroyed by fire. It was then that Sister Ursula came to America. Still a relatively young woman, she nonetheless entertained no thoughts of leaving the order she had always despised. She had become, as Sister Veronique predicted, one of them.

Once, in her late forties, she had returned to Belgium to search for her father, but she had little money and found no trace of him. It was as if, as Sister Veronique had always maintained, the man had never existed. When her funds were exhausted, Sister Ursula gave up and returned to America to live out what remained of her life among the other orphans of her order. This was her first college course, she explained, and she wanted the other students to know that she had enjoyed meeting them and reading their stories, and thanked them for helping her with hers. All of this was contained in the final paragraph of the story, an unconsciously postmodern gesture.

"This last part sort of fizzled out," one student admitted, clearly pained to say this after its author had thanked her readers for their help. "But it's one of the best stories we've read all semester."

"I liked it too," said another, whose voice didn't fall quite right.

Everyone seemed to understand that there was more to say, but no one knew what it might be. Sister Ursula stopped taking notes and silence descended on the room. For some time I'd been watching a young woman who'd said next to nothing all term, but who wrote long, detailed reports on all the stories. She'd caught my attention now because her eyes were brimming with tears. I sent her an urgent telepathic plea. No. Please don't.

"But the girl in the story never *got* it," she protested.

The other students, including Sister Ursula, all turned toward her. "Got what?"

I confess, my own heart was in my throat.

"About the father," she said. "He was the mother's pimp, right? Is there another explanation?"

"So," Sister Ursula said sadly, "I was writing what you call a fictional story after all."

It was now mid-December, my grades were due, and I was puzzling over what to do about Sister Ursula's. She had not turned in a final portfolio of revised work to be evaluated, nor had she returned to class after her final workshop, and no matter how hard I tried, I couldn't erase from my memory the image of the old nun that had haunted me for weeks, of her face coming apart in terrible recognition of the willful lie she'd told herself over a lifetime.

So I'd decided to pay her a visit at the old house where she and five other elderly nuns had been quartered now for nearly a decade in anticipation of their order's dissolution. I had brought the gift of a Christmas tree ornament, only to discover that they had no tree, unless you counted the nine-inch plastic one on the mantel in the living room. Talk about failures of imagination. In a house inhabited by infirm, elderly women, who did I suppose would have put up and decorated a tree?

Sister Ursula seemed surprised to see me standing there on her sloping porch, but she led me into a small parlor off the main hall. "We must be very still," she said softly. "Sister Patrice has fallen ill. I am her nurse, you see. I am nurse to all of them."

In the little room we took seats opposite each other across a small gateleg table. I must have looked uncomfortable, because Sister Ursula said, "You have always been very nervous of me, and you should not. What harm was in me has wasted away with my flesh."

"It's just that I was bitten by a nun as a child," I explained.

Sister Ursula, who'd said so many horrible things about nuns, looked momentarily shocked. Then she smiled. "Oh, I understand that you made a joke," she said. "I thought that you might be . . . what was that word the boy in our class used to describe those like me?"

I had to think a minute. "Oh, a misogynist?"

"Yes, that. Would you tell me the truth if I asked you do you like women?"

"Yes, I do. Very much."

"And I men, so we are the same. We each like the opposite from us."

Which made me smile. And perhaps because she had confided so much about herself, I felt a sudden, irrational urge to confide something in return. Something terrible, perhaps. Something I believed to be true. That my wife had left because she had discovered my involvement with a woman I did not love, who I had taken up with, I now realized, because I felt cheated when the book I'd published in the spring had not done well, cheated because my publisher had been irresponsibly optimistic, claiming the book would make me rich and famous, and because I'd been irresponsibly willing to believe it, so that when it provided neither fame nor fortune, I began to look around for a consolation prize and found her. I am not a good man, I might have told Sister Ursula. I have not only failed but also betrayed those I love. If I said such things to Sister Ursula, maybe she would find some inconsistency in my tale, some flaw. Maybe she'd conclude that I was judging myself too harshly and find it in her heart to say, "You don't mean that."

But I kept my truths to myself, because she was right. I *was* "nervous of her."

After an awkward moment of silence, she said, "I would like to show you something, if you would like to see it?"

Sister Ursula struggled heavily to her feet and left the room, returning almost immediately. The old photograph was pretty much as described—brown and curled at its scalloped edges, the womanly image at its center faded nearly into white. But still beautiful. It might have been the photo of a young Sister Ursula, but of course it wasn't. Since there was nothing to say, I said nothing, merely put it down on the small table between us.

"You? You had loving parents?"

I nodded. "Yes."

"You are kind. This visit is to make sure that I am all right, I understand. But I am wondering for a long time. You also knew the meaning of my story?"

I nodded.

"From the beginning?"

"No, not from the beginning."

"But the young woman was correct? Based on the things that I wrote, there could be no other . . . interpretation?"

"Not that I could see."

"And yet *I* could not see."

There was a sound then, a small, dull thud from directly overhead. "Sister Patrice," Sister Ursula informed me, and we got to our feet. "I am needed. Even a hateful nun is sometimes needed."

At the front door, I decided to ask. "One thing," I said. "The fire . . . that destroyed the school?"

Sister Ursula smiled and took my hand. "No," she assured me. "All I did was pray."

She looked off across the years, though, remembering. "Ah, but the flames," she said, her old eyes bright with a young woman's fire. "They reached almost to heaven."

Monhegan Light

Well, he'd been wrong, Martin had to admit as Monhegan began to take shape on the horizon. Wrong about the island, about the ferry. Maybe even wrong to make this journey in the first place. Joyce, Laura's sister, had implied as much, not that he'd paid much attention to her, cunt that she was. Imagine, still trying to make him feel guilty so long after the fact of Laura's death, as if *he* was the one who'd been living a lie for twenty-five years. He could still see her smirking at him. "Poor Martin," she'd said after telling him, with surprisingly little reluctance, where Robert Trevor was to be found. Almost as if she *wanted* Martin to meet the man. "You just don't get it, do you?"

Of all the things that Joyce's sort of woman said about men, Martin disliked the he-just-doesn't-get-it riff most of all. For one thing it presupposed there was something to get, usually something obvious, something you'd have to be blind not to see. And of course the reason you couldn't see it—as women were happy to explain—was that you had a dick, as if that poor, maligned appendage were constantly in a man's line of sight, blocking his view of what women, who were not similarly encumbered, wanted him to take notice of, something subtle or delicate or beautiful, at least to their way of thinking. If you didn't agree that it was subtle or delicate or beautiful, it was because you had a dick. You just didn't get it.

But he *had* been wrong about the island. He'd imagined Monhegan as harboring some sort of retreat or commune inhabited by starving, self-deluded, talentless fringe painters like Joyce. Wannabes. (Not that Robert Trevor, alas, was one of those.) But a quick scan of the brochure had shown him that he was wrong. This was no commune. The artists who summered here were not hoping to "arrive" one day; they already had. The island's other claim to fame was its hiking trails, for which he was grateful. Otherwise, how could he have explained to Beth his sudden urge to visit this particular island.

The woman in question had closed her eyes and reclined her head over the back of the seat so that her smooth throat was exposed to the weakening September sun. Her long hair hung straight down, spilling onto the top of a backpack that a young man sitting behind them had wedged between the seats. Martin gave the boy an apologetic smile, and received in return a shrug of camaraderie that suggested the boy understood about pretty women who were careless with their hair.

No, Beth was not the sort of girl, Martin reassured himself, who became suspicious. In fact, her ability to take in new data without apparent surprise was one of her great life skills. An arched eyebrow seemed to represent the extreme end of her emotional range when it came to revelation, and to Martin's way of thinking, there was much to be said for such emotional economy, especially in a woman. Beth never said I-told-you-so, even in an I-told-you-so situation, of which the ferry was the latest.

The whole trip, hastily arranged after the shoot had wrapped, was not going smoothly. Both legs of the flight east had been full, which meant they'd not been able to sit together. Martin had been of the opinion that flyers were generally happy to switch seats so that people who were traveling together could sit together, but such requests, they discovered, were far more likely to be honored in order to seat a child next to his mother than to place a middle-aged man next to his fetching, far younger traveling companion. Martin had also been of the opinion that they'd have no trouble picking up a car in Portland, having no reason to know that there was a convention in town. So, instead of heading directly up the coast, they'd spent a day in Portland in a very shabby motel waiting for a rental to become available. And now the ferry.

"I think I've discovered why they don't take cars," Martin told her, gesturing with the tourist brochure. He'd assured her yesterday that all the ferries along coastal Maine took automobiles, and that now, after Labor Day, they probably wouldn't even need a reservation. "There are no roads on the island."

Of course there was a downside to Beth's emotional reticence. That arched eyebrow of hers did manage to convey, perhaps by intention, perhaps not, that she wasn't greatly surprised if you got something wrong, because she understood you, knew you better than you knew yourself, and therefore *expected* you to be wrong about a lot of things. Glancing over at her now, Martin was rewarded with the precise arched eyebrow he'd anticipated, its meaning unmistakable. Fortunately there was also a trace of a smile, and in that smile a hint of generosity that distinguished her from professional bitches like Joyce. Both might come to the same conclusion—that you didn't get it—but only one of them held it against you.

"No paved roads, anyway," he continued, after Beth allowed her eyes to close again sleepily. "Except for the summer, there are only seventy-five full-time residents on the island. Five children attend the local school."

Beth didn't open her eyes when she spoke. "I wonder if they have a special program for gifted kids."

Martin chuckled. "Or a remedial one, come to that."

She didn't smile, causing Martin to wonder if he'd misread her remark. He'd assumed she meant it to be funny, since it was, but one never knew. "She looks perfect for you, Martin," Joyce had remarked yesterday, though Beth had remained in the car while Martin climbed the front porch steps and rang the bell. "How clever of you two to find each other."

"They suggested that visitors bring a flashlight, since power outages are pretty common," he said, looking up from the brochure. "I don't suppose you've got a flashlight on you?"

At this, Beth pulled the material of her tube top away from her chest to check. From where Martin sat, her entire right breast was exposed for a full beat before she allowed the elastic to snap back into place. The young man seated behind them had chosen that precise moment to stand up, which meant that he must have gotten an even better view.

"Hey," he whispered, once the boy had wandered over to the railing. "This ain't L.A."

"It's not?" she said, feigning astonishment. "Really?"

"Okay, fine," he said. "But people have different attitudes about things in New England." California born and bred, Martin had been to the Northeast only a couple of times, both on shoots, once to southern Connecticut, which didn't feel much like New England, and once to Boston, which felt like most other big cities. But Puritanism had flowered in this same rocky soil, hadn't it? And after driving up the coast of Maine from Portland, Martin thought he understood why people who lived in such a harsh, unforgiving landscape might come to sterner conclusions about sex and life in general than they did in, say, Malibu.

"Well, old man, I've spent a lot of money on these boobs."

Which was true. And not just her boobs either, Martin was certain. Beth was a firm believer in fixing whatever ailed you and also, come to think of it, a believer in firmness. At thirty-five her body was taut and lean, her long legs tanned and ropelike, her stomach flat from thousands of murderous crunches. Her breasts, truth be told, were a little too firm, at least for Martin, better to look at than to caress. Whatever she'd had done to them caused her nipples to be in a constant state of erection. If the boy over at the rail had gotten a good look, he'd already had the best of them.

"In California," Martin's friend Peter Axelrod was fond of saying wistfully, "ugliness is gradually being bred out of the species." And beauty along with it, Martin sometimes thought. Living in L.A. and working in "the industry," Martin saw many beautiful women, and even the most beautiful were anxious about some supposed flaw, from Audrey Hepburn's eyebrows to Meryl Streep's nose. On the set he'd witnessed many a tearful, whispered conversation in which an actress would explain how that next shot would reveal or emphasize some terrible imperfection she was determined to conceal. Axelrod, whose face had been badly burned in childhood, handled them as well as anybody. "Look at me," he'd say quietly. "Look at this face and then tell me *you're* ugly." They loved him for that, sometimes, Martin suspected, even sleeping with him out of gratitude. Back in his director's chair, he'd give the actress a few minutes to compose herself, explaining to the waiting crew, in his most confidential tones, "Everybody wants to be perfect. I certainly hope this isn't a perfect movie we're making." Whereupon he would be assured they weren't.

Strangely, when Axelrod himself wed, late in life, the woman he married might have been Beth's sister, a flawless beauty some twenty years his junior with a face and body whose perfect symmetry seemed computer-generated. Which probably meant that men, ultimately, *were* to blame. That's certainly what Joyce would say. It was men, after all, who were responsible for setting the standards of feminine beauty. Someday, Martin felt certain, it would be discovered what women were responsible for, though probably not in his lifetime.

When he looked up from his brochure, Martin saw that the island's lighthouse had come into view above the dark line of trees, so he got up and went over to the rail for a better look. A few minutes later, the ferry rounded the southernmost tip of the island and chugged into the tiny harbor with its scattering of small buildings built into the hillside. High above and blindingly white, the lighthouse was straight out of a Hopper painting, presiding over a village starkly brilliant in its detail. Martin could feel his eyes welling up in the stiff breeze, and when he felt Beth at his elbow, he tried to wipe the tear out of the corner of his left eye with the heel of his hand, a gesture he hoped looked natural. She must have noticed, though, because she said, "Don't be jealous, babe. God lit this one."

It wasn't until they'd disembarked from the ferry, until they located their bags on the dock and started up the hill toward the second-best accommodations on the island, that Martin turned back and saw the name painted on the ferry's transom: *The Laura B.*

He'd told Beth nothing of his wife, except that she'd died several years ago and that they'd stayed married, he supposed, out of inertia. Beth seemed content with this slender account, but she rarely wanted more information than Martin had already offered about most anything. He would have concluded that she was genuinely incurious except that sometimes, if he'd been particularly evasive, she'd pose a follow-up question, days or even weeks after the fact, as if it had taken her all that time to realize he'd not been terribly forthcoming. Worse, she always remembered his precise words, which meant he couldn't plead misunderstanding when a subject got unpleasantly revisited. Often her questions took the form of statements, as was the case now.

"That woman didn't appear to like you very much," she observed over her chicken Caesar salad.

They were the only two people in the dining room. They'd checked in just after two and were told that the dining room was closed, though the young woman working in the kitchen said she supposed, inasmuch as they were guests of the hotel, they might be fed something if what they wanted wasn't too complicated. Martin had ordered a bowl of chowder, figuring something of that sort was probably what the woman had in mind. Beth had ordered the chicken Caesar, which was what she would have ordered if the woman had been mute on the subject of what they might and might not have. When she brought their food a few minutes later, the woman said that the last seating for dinner would be at seven-thirty, which either registered or not with Beth, who didn't look up from the trail map she was studying. She'd changed into hiking clothes in their room.

Martin was about to remark that it was Beth herself whom the cook wasn't fond of when it occurred to him that she'd been referring to Joyce.

"She was Laura's sister," he said, as if it was common

knowledge that all sisters despised their brothers-in-law by natural decree.

"Did you fuck her?" Beth asked around a bite of blackened chicken breast.

"Joyce?" Martin snorted.

"Well, I assume you were fucking your wife," Beth pointed out, not unreasonably. Martin might have corrected her, but did not. "Besides, men have been known—"

"I'll try to forgive that unkind and entirely unwarranted suspicion," he said, blowing on his chowder, the first spoon of which had burned his tongue.

"This is an excellent Caesar salad," Beth said.

"Good," he told her. "I'm glad."

"Now you're mad at me."

"No."

"Tell me," she said, leaving him to wonder for a full beat whether she intended to change the subject or forge ahead. Change it, was Martin's guess, and he was right. "What will you be doing while I'm climbing the island's dangerous cliffs, which this publication warns me not to do alone?"

He decided not to take this particular bait. "I thought I'd take some pictures, maybe visit a gallery or two. See if I can locate a bottle of wine for dinner." The hotel, they'd been informed upon checking in, had no liquor license.

"One dinner without wine wouldn't kill us, actually," Beth said.

"How do you know?"

"Well, it's true I'm only guessing."

Martin studied her until she pushed her plate away. As usual, about half her food was untouched. In all of the time they'd been together, nearly a year now, Martin had never known her to finish a serving of anything. In restaurants known for small portions, Beth would order twice as much food and still leave half. Laura, he recalled, had eaten like a man, with appetite and appreciation.

Then a thought struck him. "When have I ever been unable to answer the bell?" he asked. "Any bell."

Beth gave him a small smile, which meant that their argument, if that's what this was, was over. "I'm not overly fond of boxing metaphors applied to sex," she said, taking one of his thumbs and pulling on it. "It's not war."

Like hell, Martin thought.

"But yes," she conceded, "you *do* answer every bell, old man."

"Thank you," Martin said, meaning it. The question he'd asked had been risky, he realized, and he was glad the danger had passed.

"I'm going back to the room for some sunscreen," she said, pushing her chair back. "I'll be taking the 'A' Trail—"

Martin whistled a few bars of "Take the 'A' Train."

"—in case I need rescuing."

Watching her cross the room, he had a pretty good idea what the sunscreen was for. She'd sunbathe on a rock, topless, in some secluded spot, while the young fellow from the ferry scrutinized her through binoculars from an adjacent bluff. *You could go with her,* he said to himself. *There's nothing preventing you.*

But there was.

. . .

From what he'd read in the brochure, roughly a third of the houses on the island had to be artists' studios, though to the casual eye they looked no different from the other houses inhabited, presumably, by lobstermen and the owners of the island's few seasonal businesses. All of the buildings were sided with the same weathered gray shingles, as if subjected, decades ago, to a dress code. He'd half expected to discover that Joyce had lied to him, but Robert Trevor's studio was right where she said it would be, at the edge of the village where the dirt road ended and one of the island's dozen or so hiking trails began. Martin had watched Beth disappear up another of these half an hour ago, purposely waiting until he was sure she hadn't forgotten something and wouldn't return until early evening.

Trevor's studio was unmarked except for a tiny sign with his last name to the left of the door, which was open. Martin was about to knock on the screen door when he heard a loud crash from around back of the house. There, on the elevated deck, Martin found a large man with a flowing mane of silver hair, dressed in paint-splattered jeans and an unbuttoned denim work shirt. He was teetering awkwardly on one knee, his other leg stretched out stiffly in front of him like a prosthesis, trying to prop up a rickety three-legged table with its splintered fourth leg. Jelly jars and paintbrushes were strewn everywhere. One small jar, which according to its label had originally contained artichoke hearts, had described a long, wet arc over the sloping deck and come to a teetering pause at the top of the steps before thumping down all five, coming to rest at Martin's feet.

He picked it up and waited for Robert Trevor—clearly this man was the artist himself—to take notice of him. The wooden leg fell off again as soon as the man, with considerable difficulty, got back to his feet and tested the table. "All right, be that way," he said, tossing the leg aside and collapsing into a chair that didn't look much sturdier than the table. It groaned under his considerable weight, but ultimately held. Martin saw that Robert Trevor was sweating and his forehead was smudged with several different colors of paint from his palette. There was an easel set up next to the table, and Trevor studied the half-finished canvas resting there, a landscape, as if rickety furniture were the least of his problems.

It took him a minute to sense Martin's presence at the foot of his deck, and even then he didn't react with as much surprise as Martin himself would have displayed had their situations been reversed. The painter nodded at Martin as if he'd been expecting him, and he did not get up. "You," he said, running his fingers through his hair, "would be Laura's husband."

"Martin."

"Right, Martin."

"Joyce called you?"

Trevor snorted. "I don't have a phone. That's one of the many beauties of this place." He paused to let this vaguely political observation sink in. "No, the sun went behind a cloud and I looked over and there you were. I made the connection."

Okay, Martin thought. So that's the way it's going to be.

The sun *had* disappeared behind a cloud in that instant, and Martin thought of Beth walking along the cliffs on the back side of the island. She'd be disappointed now, lacking an excuse to sunbathe topless.

"I'm going to need that, Martin," the painter told him, indicating the artichoke jar.

"Can I come up?" Martin asked.

"Have you come to murder me?" Trevor asked. "Did you bring a gun?"

Martin shook his head. "No, no gun. I just came to have a look at you," he said, pleased that this statement so nicely counterbalanced in its unpleasantness the painter's own remark about the sun.

Trevor apparently appreciated the measured response as well. "Well, I guess I'll have to trust you," he replied, finally struggling to his feet.

Martin climbed the steps to the deck, where there was an awkward moment since neither man seemed to relish the notion of shaking hands.

"There's another of those jars under the table, if you feel nimble," the man said. "I could do it myself but it would take me an hour."

Martin fetched that jar and two others while Trevor picked up his brushes, arranging them in groupings that made no sense to Martin, then added solvent to each of the jars from a tin can. Martin, crouching low, managed to wedge the leg back in place fairly securely, then stood up.

"I didn't mean for you to stop work," he said, realizing that this was what was happening.

The painter regarded him as if he'd said something particularly foolish. He was a very big man, Martin couldn't help but notice; he had a huge belly, but was tall enough to carry the weight without appearing obese. He'd probably been slimmer before, when he and Laura were lovers. Martin hadn't doubted that this was what they were from the moment he unpacked the painting.

"The light's about finished for today, Martin," the other man shrugged. "The best light's usually early. The rest is memory. Not like that bastard business you're in."

So, Martin thought. Laura had talked about them. First she'd fucked this painter and then she'd told him about their marriage and their lives.

"What's that term movie people use for the last good light of the day?"

"Magic hour?"

"Right. Magic hour," Trevor nodded. "Tell me, is that real, or just something you people made up?"

"It's real enough."

"Real enough," Trevor repeated noncommittally, as if to weigh the implications of "enough." "Well, if you aren't here to murder me, why don't you have a seat while I get us a beer. And when I come back, you can tell me if *my* Laura's 'real enough' to suit you."

She had arrived professionally wrapped and crated, and when Martin saw the return address on the label, he set the parcel aside in the corner of his study. Joyce had always been an unpleasant woman, so it stood to reason that whatever she was sending him would be unpleasant. She'd called a week earlier, telling him to expect something but refusing to say what. "I wouldn't be sending it," she explained, "except I hear you have a new girlfriend. Is it serious, Martin?"

"I don't see where it's any of your business, Joyce," he'd told her, glad to have this to say since he didn't have any idea whether he and Beth were serious or not. Still, it was something of a mystery how Joyce, who lived clear across the country, could have heard about Beth to begin with. Why she should care was another. What she'd sent him, crated so expertly against the possibility of damage, was a third, but all three mysteries together aroused little curiosity in Martin. That the parcel contained a painting was obvious from its shape and packaging, but he'd idly assumed that talentless, bitter Joyce herself was the painter.

So he'd left the package unopened for more than a week. Beth had been curious about it, or maybe just intrigued by his own lack of interest. She loved presents and received a great many, it seemed to Martin, although the majority were from her doting father, a man not much older than Martin himself. Daddy, as she referred to him, lived in Minnesota with a wife his own age, and Martin, thankfully, had never met either of them. Beth displayed little urgent affection for her parents, though her eyes always lit up when one of her father's packages arrived. "You never buy me presents, Martin," she sometimes said, feigning complaint, when she opened one of these. "Why is that?"

Whatever instinct prevented Martin from opening the painting in front of Beth, he was grateful for it as soon as he tore the outer covering off the skeleton of protective latticework. Seeing Laura there, just behind the cross-hatched slats, he had to suppress a powerful urge to lock the front door and pull the curtains shut against the brilliant California sunlight. After she was uncrated and leaning against the wall, he'd remained transfixed for a long time—he couldn't afterward be sure how long—and for almost as long by Robert Trevor's signature in the lower right of the canvas. He didn't need the signature, of course, to know that Joyce was not the painter. She hadn't anything like this measure of talent, for one thing. For another, she never would've seen Laura like this. It wasn't just his wife's nakedness, or even her pose, just inside an open doorway, light streaming in on her, all other objects disappearing into shadow. It was something else. The painting's detail was minutely photographic where the light allowed, yet it was very much "painted," interpreted, Martin supposed, an effect no camera eye could achieve. Joyce would've gotten a charge out of it, he had to admit, when the spell finally broke. The sight of him kneeling before Laura would have covered both her trouble and the expense.

"So what was it?" Beth asked when she returned from work that evening. He'd opened a bottle of white wine and drunk half of it before he heard the garage door grind open and Beth's Audi pull inside.

"What was *what*?" he said, affecting nonchalance.

She poured herself a glass of the wine, regarded him strangely, then held up a splintered slat from the latticework he'd broken into small pieces over his knee and stuffed into one of the large rubber trash cans they kept in the garage. Had he forgotten to put the lid on? Or was it Beth's habit to examine the trash on her way in each evening, to see if he'd thrown away anything interesting?

"Something hateful," he finally said, believing this to be true, then adding, "Nothing important," as pure a lie as he'd ever told.

She nodded, as if this explanation were sufficient and holding her wineglass up to the light. "Not our usual white," she remarked, after taking a sip.

"No."

"A hint of sweet. You usually hate that."

"Let's go to Palm Springs for the weekend," he suggested.

She continued to study him, now clearly puzzled. "You just finished shooting in Palm Springs. You said you hated it."

"It'll be different now," he explained, "with us gone."

"So, Martin," Trevor said when he returned with two bottles of sweating domestic beer, a brand Martin didn't realize was even brewed anymore. He'd partially buttoned his blue denim work shirt, Martin noticed, though a tuft of gray, paint-splattered chest hair was still visible at the open neck. The man sat in stages, as if negotiating with the lower half of his body. "Have I seen any of your films?"

"*My* films?" Martin smiled, then took a swallow of cold, bitter beer. "I'm not a director, Robert."

The man was still trying to get settled, lifting his bad

leg straight out in front of him by hand, clearly annoyed by the need to do so. "When I was inside, I was trying to remember the word for what you are. Laura told me, but I forgot."

"Cuckold?" Martin suggested.

Robert Trevor didn't respond right away. This was a man whose equilibrium did not tilt easily, and Martin found himself admiring that. His eyes were a piercing, pale blue. Laura, naked, had allowed him to turn them on her. "Now *there's* a Renaissance word for you," Trevor said finally. "A Renaissance notion, actually."

"You think so?" Martin said, pressing what he felt should have been his advantage. "Have you ever been married, Robert?"

"Never," the painter admitted. "Flawed concept, I always thought."

"Some might say it's people who are flawed, not the concept."

Robert Trevor looked off in the distance as if he were considering the merit of Martin's observation, but then he said, "Gaffer! That's what you are. You're a gaffer."

Martin had to restrain a smile. Clearly, if he'd come all this way in hopes of an apology, he was going to be disappointed. The good news was that this was not—he was pretty sure—what he had come for.

"Laura explained it all to me one afternoon," Trevor explained.

"Actually, I'm a D.P. now," Martin said, and was immediately ashamed of his need to explain that he'd come up in the world.

Trevor frowned. "Dip?" he said. "You're a dip, Martin?"

"Director of photography."

"Ah," the other man said. "I guess that makes you an artist."

"No," Martin said quietly. "Merely a technician."

He'd been called an artist, though. Peter Axelrod considered him one. He'd gotten an urgent call from Peter one night a few years ago, asking Martin to come to the set where he was shooting a picture that starred a famously difficult actor. It was a small film, serious in content and intent, and for the first three weeks the director and star had been embroiled in a quiet struggle. The actor was determined to give a performance that would be hailed as masterfully understated. To Peter's way of thinking, his performance, to this point, was barely implied. Worse, the next day they'd be shooting one of the pivotal scenes.

Martin found his old friend sitting alone in a makeshift theater near the set, morosely studying the dailies. Martin took a seat in the folding chair next to him and together they watched take after take. After half an hour, Peter called for the lights. "There's nothing to choose from," he complained, rubbing his forehead. "He does the same thing every fucking take, no matter what I suggest."

To Martin, perhaps because he could focus on one thing while his friend had to juggle fifty, the problem was obvious. "Don't argue with him. He's just going to dig his heels in deeper, the way they all do. You want a star performance, light him like a star, not like a character actor."

Peter considered this advice for all of about five seconds. "Son of a *bitch*," he said. "David's in cahoots with him, isn't he." David, a man Martin knew well, was Peter's D.P. on the film. "I should shit-can the prick and hire you right this second."

Martin, of course, had demurred. The following week he was starting work on another picture, and Peter's offer wasn't so much literal as symbolic, a token to his gratitude. "You just saved this picture," he told Martin out on the lot. "In fact, you just saved me."

The two men were shaking hands then, when Peter remembered. "I was sorry to hear about Laura," he said, looking stricken. "It must have been awful."

"Pretty bad," Martin admitted. "She weighed about eighty pounds at the end."

The two men looked around the lot. "Movies," the director said, shaking his head. "I wonder what we'd have done if we'd decided to live real lives and have real careers."

"You love movies," Martin pointed out.

"I know," Peter had admitted. "God help me, I do."

"Merely a technician," Trevor repeated now, improbably seated across from Martin on the opposite coast. He'd already drained half his beer, while Martin, never a beer drinker, had barely touched his. "Well, I wouldn't worry about it. In the end, maybe that's all art is. Solid technique with a dash of style."

"I don't much feel like talking about aesthetics, Robert."

"No, I don't suppose you do," the painter said, running his fingers through his hair. "Joyce told me she sent you that painting. I'd have tried to talk her out of that, had I known."

"Why?"

"Because Laura wouldn't have wanted her to. Funny to think of them as sisters, actually. Joyce always seeking vengeance. Laura anxious to forgive."

Which was true. Martin had seen photos of them as little girls, when it was hard to tell them apart. But by adolescence Laura was already flowering into the healthy, full-figured, ruddily complected woman she would become, whereas Joyce, pale and thin, had begun to look out at the world through dark, aggrieved eyes. When Martin had seen her yesterday, it was clear that not one of her myriad grievances had ever been addressed to her satisfaction.

"So, Robert. How long were you and my wife lovers?"

Trevor paused, deciding how best, or perhaps whether, to answer. "Why would you want to know that, Martin? How will knowing make anything better?"

"How long?"

After a beat, the painter said, "We had roughly twenty years' worth of summers."

Right, Martin thought. The worst, then. Odd that he couldn't remember whether Laura had ever directly deceived him, or whether she'd simply allowed him to deceive himself. He'd assumed that she needed this time with her sister each summer. That she never asked him to come along, given his opinion of Joyce, he'd considered a kindness.

"A month one year. Six weeks the next. I painted her every minute I could, then kept at it when she was gone."

Yes. The worst. This was one of the things he'd needed to know, of course. "How many are there?"

"Paintings?" Trevor asked. "A dozen finished oils. More watercolors. Hundreds of studies. The one Joyce sent you might be the best of the lot. You should hang on to it."

"Where are they?" he asked, then nodded at the studio. "Here?"

"At my farm in Indiana."

"You never sold any of them?"

"I've never *shown* any of them."

"Why not?"

"She wouldn't allow it when she was alive. Joyce kept the one you have in the guest room Laura used when she visited. Laura made her promise never to show anyone."

"She's been dead for several years now."

"Also, there were your feelings to consider."

Martin snorted. "Please. You want me to believe you gave that a lot of thought?"

"Not even remotely," Trevor admitted. "Laura did, though. And . . . after her death . . . I starting thinking of the pictures as private. When I die will be time enough."

"So nobody knows about them?"

"You do. Joyce. My New York agent *suspects,* and I've given instructions concerning them to my attorney." He finished his beer, then peered into the bottle as if, there at the bottom, the names of others who knew about the paintings might be printed. "That's what you should prepare yourself for, Martin. I've never pursued fame, but it appears I've become famous anyway, at least in certain circles. When I die, Laura's going to become a very famous lady. Everybody loves a secret. In fact"—at this he smiled and put the bottle down, turning to look at Martin—"you might want to option the movie rights."

"Did you know she was dying?"

"She told me when she was first diagnosed, yes. I painted her that summer, like always."

Martin massaged his temples, the tips of his fingers cool from holding the beer bottle.

"She insisted. And of course I wanted to. I couldn't not paint her. I would have, right to the end, had that been possible."

"Why?"

"Why paint her disease, you mean?"

No, that wasn't what he'd meant, not exactly, though he was ashamed to articulate further. "Why paint her at all, Robert? That's what I've been wondering. She wasn't what you'd call a beautiful woman."

Trevor didn't hesitate at all. "No, Martin, she wasn't what *you'd* call a beautiful woman. She was one of the most beautiful women *I've* ever laid eyes on."

Yes, Martin thought. That was obvious from the moment he'd opened the crate. And his next question was the reason he'd come so far. "Why?" he heard himself ask. "What was it about her?"

"I thought you didn't want to talk about aesthetics, Martin," the painter replied.

That night, Martin and Beth ate by candlelight in the inn's small dining room. The candles were a matter of necessity. The storm had blown up out of nowhere, or so

47

it seemed to Martin. The sun had disappeared behind that first cloud when he'd arrived at Trevor's studio; by the time he'd left, an hour later, the sky was rumbling with dark, low thunderheads from horizon to horizon. The painter, predicting that the island would lose power, had insisted that Martin take a flashlight with him. "Just leave it in the room," he'd instructed. "I run into Dennis and Pat all the time. They can return it whenever." When Martin smiled at this and shook his head, Trevor read his thought and nodded in agreement. "Island life, Martin. Island life."

He had walked with Martin as far as the gate, an effort that clearly cost him. "What's wrong with your leg, Robert?" Martin asked as he lifted the latch to let himself out.

"It's my hip, actually. It needs replacing, they tell me. I'm thinking about it."

Martin remembered the battered table Trevor used for his paints, the broken leg he continued to prop under it. Unless he was very much mistaken, Trevor wasn't the sort of man who put much faith in "replacement."

"You didn't come to visit her," Martin remarked—one last-ditch attempt at censure—after the gate swung shut between them.

"No."

"You could have," he said. "You could have shown up with Joyce, claimed to be an old friend. I wouldn't have known."

"I thought about it," Trevor admitted. "But I had it on excellent authority that I wasn't needed. You rose to the occasion, is what I heard."

In the distance, a low rumble of thunder.

"That's what our friend Joyce can't quite forgive you for, by the way," he continued. "Your devotion during those last months enraged her. Up to that point, she'd always felt perfectly justified in despising you."

"You mean I rose to the occasion of her death, but not her life?"

"Something like that," Trevor nodded. "But look at it this way. You got a damn good painting out of that woman's need to punish you."

"I don't know what to do with it, though," Martin said. "I had to rent one of those self-storage units out in the valley."

"Air-conditioned, I hope."

Martin smiled. "It's the only thing in there."

"I'd love to have it back, if you don't want it."

"It'll be even harder to look at now," he'd admitted, though he knew he'd never return the painting to Trevor. "That look of longing on her face. The way she was standing there. I'm always going to know it was you she wanted to come through that door."

"Wrong again, Martin." Trevor was leaning heavily with both hands on the gate now, letting Martin know that a handshake wasn't any more necessary now than it had been earlier. It suddenly dawned on Martin that the man had to be in his seventies. "I was the one who *did* come through that door. You were the one she was waiting for."

"So," Beth said, digging into her steak with genuine appetite. At least, Martin thought, she wasn't one of those

L.A. girls who always order fish and drink nothing but mineral water. "Were you worried about me?"

"Yes," he said. He'd been waiting for her in a rocking chair on the inn's front porch, the sky growing blacker and blacker, when she came striding down the dirt path. She'd no more than sat down next to him than the air sizzled with electricity and the first bolt of lightning cleaved the sky.

"You forget I'm from Minnesota," she said, pointing her fork at him. "I spent the first twenty years of my life watching storms. And how was your lazy afternoon, old man?"

"Fine."

"Just fine?"

"I visited a studio. Took some photos. Like I said."

"You should've come with me. The path through the forest is strewn with fairy houses."

"With what?"

"Little houses built of bark and leaves and pebbles. By children, I suppose, if you don't believe in fairies. People leave pennies near the ones they like best. Isn't that sweet? I can see why Laura loved it here."

Martin just stared at her.

"Well . . . that's why we came all this way, right? This island was your wife's favorite place in the whole world, and this is your way of saying goodbye."

"I didn't know you—"

"I'm not *stupid*, Martin. I know how much you loved her."

But I didn't. The words were right there to be spoken, and for a heartbeat Martin thought he'd already said them. But if he did, how would he ever stop? How would he keep from adding, *Any more than I love you.*

They used Robert Trevor's flashlight to wind their way up the narrow, pitch-black staircase to locate their room on the third floor. Undressing in the dark, they lay in the canopied bed and watched the sky through the open window. Though the storm had moved out to sea, it still flickered on the distant horizon, and every twenty seconds or so the beam from the lighthouse swept past.

"What do you think?" Beth said. "Should we stay an extra day?"

"If you like," he said. "Whatever you want."

"It's up to you."

After a moment he said, "I called Peter while you were out. He needs me to start work earlier, by the second week of rehearsal instead of the third, if possible. He didn't come right out and say so, but that's what he wants."

"What do *you* want?"

"I wouldn't mind heading back."

"Fine with me."

"Let's, then."

A few minutes later she was snoring gently in the crook of his arm. For a long time Martin lay in the dark thinking about Robert Trevor's farm in Indiana, if there was such a place, and the countless versions of Laura he claimed to have stored there. And he thought too about Beth, the poor girl. She had it exactly backwards, of course. This trip wasn't so much about saying goodbye to his wife as saying hello. He'd fallen in love with her, truly in love, the moment he'd uncrated the painting back in L.A. and seen his wife through another man's eyes. Just as Joyce had known, somehow, that he would.

What folly, Martin couldn't help concluding, bitterly, as he contemplated the lovely young woman sleeping at his side; it was his destiny, no doubt, to sell her short as well. What absolute folly love was. Talk about a flawed concept. He remembered how he and his junior high friends—all of them shy, self-conscious, without girlfriends—used to congregate in the shadow of the bleachers to evaluate the girls at Friday night dances. The best ones were taken, naturally, which left the rest. "She's kind of pretty, don't you think?" one of his friends, or maybe Martin himself, would venture, and then it would be decided, by popular consensus, if she was or she wasn't.

That they were leaving in the morning was a relief to Martin. He preferred the West Coast, and he was looking forward to working on Peter's new picture, which was to star an actress they'd both worked with shortly after Laura's death. That script had called for partial nudity, and the actress, who'd recently had a baby, fretted constantly about how she would look. "Trust me," Peter had told her. "Nobody's going to see anything. They're just going to think they do. Because this man"—he pointed to Martin—"is an artist."

The next evening, the three of them sat on folding chairs watching the dailies of the scene that had so frightened her. They'd shot only three takes, and midway through viewing the first the actress—she *was* one of the most beautiful women Martin had ever laid eyes on, and never more beautiful than right then—began to relax, intuiting that it was going to be all right. Still, he couldn't have been more surprised when she took his hand there in the darkness, leaned toward him and whispered, without ever taking her eyes off the screen, "Oh, I love you, I love you, I love you."

The Farther You Go

I've cut only a couple of swaths when I have to shut the damn thing down because of the pain. It's not dagger pain, but deep, rumbling, nausea pain, the sort that seems to radiate in waves from the center of my being. There are those who think that a man's phallus *is* the center of his being, but I have not been among them until now.

From inside the house Faye heard me shut off the mower, and now she's come out onto the deck to see why. She shades her eyes with a small hand, scout fashion, to see me better, though the sun is behind her. Ours is a large yard and I'm a long way off. "What's wrong?" she calls.

I'd like to tell her. It's a question she's asked on and off for thirty years, and just once I'd like to answer it. *My dick is throbbing,* I'd like to call out, and if we had any neighbors within hearing, I believe I would, so help me. But to prevent that we've bought two adjacent lots. Regrets? I've had a few. I mow their yards and my own.

"Nothing," I call to Faye. It's my standard line. Nothing is wrong. Go ahead, just try to find something that's wrong. If something were wrong, I constantly assure her, I'd say so, always amazed at how readily this lie springs to my lips. I've never in my life told her when anything was wrong, and I have no intention of telling her about my throbbing groin now. She already spent a thousand dollars we didn't really have on a riding mower simply because the doctor insisted I not "overdo it" so soon after the operation. It didn't occur to her that for a man recovering from prostate surgery, sitting on top of a vibrating engine might not be preferable to gently guiding a self-propelled mower. I can hardly blame her for this failure of imagination since it didn't occur to me either until I was aboard and in gear.

I start up the mower again and cut a long loop back to the base of the deck, stopping directly below her and turning the engine off for good.

"You're finished?"

"You can't tell?" I say, looking back over the yard. I appear to have cut a warning track around a fenceless outfield, and am now sitting on home plate.

"Why are you perspiring?"

It's true. There is autumn in the air, and no reason whatsoever to be sweating, cast about as I might. "It's a beauty," I say, slapping the steering wheel affectionately. "Worth every penny. How much was it again?"

"I just got off the phone with Julie," she says.

This does not sound good to me. Our daughter seldom

calls without a reason. She and her husband, Russell, owe us too much money to enjoy casual conversation. They're building a house half a mile up the road from our own. "Where?" I asked last year after Faye broke the news that they'd purchased a lot. "Here? In Connecticut? In *Durham*?" I was certain that some kind of trust had been violated. Could it be that we'd loaned them the money without a distance clause in the contract? We'd been prudent enough to ensure against neighbors on either side, but we were so focused on the threat of strangers that we failed to take family into account. Another failure of imagination.

Faye bends over the railing and holds out a delicate hand for me—half grateful, half suspicious—to take. "I know this is the last thing in the world you need, but I think you should go over there. Today," she adds, in case there's a shred of doubt in my mind that whatever this is about, it's serious.

"What," I say.

Now that she has my attention, she seems reluctant to do anything with it. She's looking for the right way to say it, and there is no right way. I can tell that much by looking at her.

"Julie says . . . Russell hit her."

I am shocked, though I've known for some time that their marriage was in trouble. To make matters worse, Russell has recently quit a good job for what he thought would be a better one, only to find that several large loans needed to start up the project he's to direct have not, as promised, been approved. It could be weeks, he admits. Months.

"I'm not sure I believe Russell would hit Julie," I tell Faye.

"I do," she says in a way that makes me believe it too. When my wife is dead sure, she's seldom wrong, except where I'm concerned.

"What am *I* supposed to do? Hit *him*?"

"She just wants to see you."

"I'm right here."

"She thinks you'll be angry."

"I *am* angry."

"No, that she didn't come to see you in the hospital. She feels guilty."

"She didn't know I'd be grateful?"

"She thought you'd be hurt. Like you were. Like I was."

"Thirty years we've been married and you still confuse me with yourself," I tell her. "I didn't want Julie at the hospital. I didn't want *you* at the hospital. Heart surgery would've been a different story."

"There are times I think you could use heart surgery. A transplant, maybe. This is our daughter we're talking about."

"One of our daughters," I correct her. "The other one is fine. So's our son."

"So is Julie."

I would like to believe her, but I'm not so sure. Before the wedding, I'd wanted to take Russell aside and ask him if he knew what he was doing. In time Julie might turn out fine, as well as the other two, but she somehow wasn't quite ripe yet. Not for the colleges she'd been in and out of. Not for a husband. Not for adult life.

As I am not ripe for intervention. My daughter may not be an adult, but she's acting like one—getting married, having houses built, borrowing money. And I don't, on general principle, like the idea of trespassing once people have slept together, because they know things about each other that you can't, and if you think you're ever going to understand what's eating them, you're a fool, even if one of them happens to be your own daughter. Especially if one of them happens to be your own daughter.

"We cannot tolerate physical abuse," Faye says. "You know I'm fond of Russell, and it may not be all his fault, but if they're out of control, we have to do something. We could end up wishing we had."

I would still like to debate the point. Even as Faye has been speaking, I've been marshaling semivalid reasons for butting out of our daughter's marriage. There are half a dozen pretty good ones, but I'd be wasting my breath.

"Julie thinks they should separate. For a while, anyway," Faye says. "That makes sense to me. She wants to insist, and she wants you to be there."

I'm not thinking of Julie now but of my own parents. If I want your help, I'll call you in, I remember telling my father during the early days of my own marriage when we had no money and things seemed worse than they really were. Maybe it's that way with Julie and Russell. Maybe things seem worse than they are. I wish for that to be the case, almost as fervently as I wish I hadn't been called in. But I have been.

I start out on foot, explaining to Faye the exercise will do me good, though in truth I just don't want to sit on top of another motor. Julie and Russell's house is only a half mile up the road, and up until the operation I'd been running two miles a day—usually in the opposite direction. Seeing their house rise up out of the ground has been an unsettling experience, though for some time it did not occur to me why, even when I saw the frame. Only when the two decks were complete—front and back—did it dawn on me why they'd wanted to use my contractor. My daughter is building my house.

"Well of course they are," Faye said when I voiced this suspicion. "You should be flattered."

"I should?" I said, wondering exactly when it was that I'd stopped being the one who saw things first.

"Theft being the sincerest form of flattery. Besides, they're a mile away. It's not like people are going to think it's a subdivision."

"Half a mile," I said. "And what bothers me is that Julie would *want* to build our house."

Their mission tile is already visible, but halfway up the hill I have to stop and let the nausea pass. Off to the side of the road there's a big flat rock that looks like a feather bed, so I go over and stretch out. It takes every bit of willpower I can muster not to unzip and check things out. Instead, I lie still and watch the moving sky. When I finally stand up again, I'm not sure I can make it the rest of the way, though this is the same hill I was running up a few months ago when I was fifty-one. Now I'm fifty-two and scared that maybe I won't be running up that many more hills. The doctors have told me they got what they were after, but I'm aware of just how little the same assurances meant in my father's case. After the chemotherapy, they sent him home with a clean bill of health and he was dead in two months.

Nevertheless, I do make the top of the hill. Up close, the house looks like a parody, but that's not Julie and Russell's fault. They simply ran out of money—their own, ours, the bank's. The grounds aren't landscaped and the winding drive is unpaved. There are patches of grass and larger patches of dirt. Not wanting to ring the doorbell, I go around back, hoping to catch sight of Julie in the kitchen. I want to talk to her first, before Russell, though I have no idea what I will say. I'm hoping that in the past half hour she will have changed her mind about inviting me into their lives. Maybe I'll see her at the window and she'll flash me a sign. I'm willing to interpret almost any gesture as meaning that I should go straight back home.

Around back, I remember there are no steps up to the deck, which is uniformly three feet off the ground on all sides. I'm looking around for a makeshift ladder when Julie comes out onto the deck, sliding the glass door shut behind her. Except for not knowing how I might join her up there, my plan seems to be working.

"I didn't think you were coming," she says.

"Hand me one of those deck chairs," I tell her.

She does, and I step up onto it. When she offers a hand, I take that too, putting my other one on the rail to heave myself up. Julie is wearing a peasant blouse, and when she leans over I see that she is wearing no brassiere. There have been other times when, against my will, I have been subjected to the sight of my daughter's bare breasts, and I wonder if this casual attitude of hers might be one of the problems she has with Russell. He might not like the idea of his friends becoming so intimately acquainted with her person over the onion dip. According to Faye, Karen, our oldest, has always kept one lone brassiere handy around the house for our visits. There is much to be said for hypocrisy.

"He's asleep on the sofa," Julie says. "Neither of us slept much last night. He finally zonked."

She smiles weakly, and when she turns full-face, I get a better view of her eye, which sports a mouse. The cheek beneath is swollen, but so is the other, perhaps from crying. Her complexion, which a year ago had finally begun to clear up, is bad again. Then, suddenly, she's in my arms and I can't think about anything but the fact that she is my daughter. If I'm not going to be much good at blaming Russell, at least I'm certain where my loyalties must be, where they have always been.

Finally, she snuffs her nose and steps back. "I've gotten some of his things together. He can pack them himself."

"You're sure about this?"

"I know I should be the one to tell him—"

"But you want me to," I finish for her. "Stay out here then."

She promises, snuffs again. I go in through the sliding door.

I know right where to find Russell. It's my house they're living in, after all, and their sofa is right where ours is. Russell, in jeans and a sweatshirt, is sitting up and rubbing his eyes when I come in. Oddly enough, he looks glad to see me.

"Hank," he says. "You don't look so hot."

"You're the first to notice," I tell him. He wants to shake hands and I see no reason not to.

"I shouldn't be sleeping in the daytime," he says, with what sounds like real guilt.

Or punching my daughter, I consider saying. But there's no need, because it's beginning to dawn on him that my unexpected appearance in his living room is not mere happenstance. He peers out through the kitchen window. Only Julie's blond head is visible on the deck outside.

"So," he says, "you're here to read me the riot act."

"Russell," I say, suddenly aware of how absurd this situation is. "I'm here to run you out of town."

"What do you mean?"

"I mean I'm going to give you a lift to the airport."

"You can't mean that."

"Russell, I do."

A car pulls up outside and we both look to see who it is, probably because whoever it is will upset the balance of our conflict. One of us will have an ally. I do not expect it to be Faye, but that's who it is, and when Russell sees this, his face falls, as if my wife's mere presence has convinced him that I am fully vested and authorized to banish him from his own property.

When Faye rings the bell, I open the door and tell her to go around back and join Julie. She wants to know how things are going. I say I just got here. How could I have just got here, she wants to know. I tell her to go around back.

"This is nuts," Russell says.

There's nothing to do but agree, so I do, and then I tell him that Julie has gathered a few of his belongings and he should get packing. Russell looks like he can't decide whether to cry or fly into a rage, but to my surprise he does as he's told.

Once he's gone off down the hall, I realize that with Julie and Faye out back, I have no one to talk to and nothing to do. It seems wrong to turn on the TV or browse through their books. I can hear Russell in the closet of one of their bedrooms, and I figure he's looking for either a suitcase or a gun. I sit down to wait, then remember something and get up. Julie has helped her mother up onto the deck and is crying again. I study the pair of them before stepping back outside. From the rear they look remarkably similar, almost like sisters. I look for something of myself in Julie and find precious little. When Faye notices me standing there at the window, I join them on the deck.

"How much do you have in your checking account?" I ask our daughter.

She blinks.

"How much?" I say.

"Not a lot," she says. "There's never much. A couple hundred dollars maybe."

"Write me a check," I say. "I'll take him to the airport."

"You want me to pay for it?" Julie says.

"You want *me* to?"

"Hank—" Faye starts.

But I'm not about to budge on this one. I'll loan her money later, or give it to her if I have to, but if she wants

Russell on a plane, she's going to experience at least the appearance of paying for it.

Julie fetches the checkbook from the drawer in the kitchen. Though she hates the idea, she writes the check anyway. I look it over, then slip it in my pocket.

"He's at the bedroom window staring at us," Julie whispers. "Don't look."

I don't intend to.

It's forty-five minutes to Bradley International. I tell Russell to take it easy. After all, it's not like we're trying to catch any particular flight. Where I will send Russell is one of the many things we have not discussed. Why he has struck my daughter is another. More than anything, I'm afraid he'll tell me what's wrong with my daughter, and why their lives together went wrong.

I know too much already. Knew, in fact, as soon as I saw my house taking shape on their lot, knowing that this wasn't Russell's idea, that if Russell had his way they'd be living in New Haven in an apartment, spending their money in restaurants, on the occasional train into New York, the theater, maybe, or a cruise around the island. The sort of things you have a ticket stub to show for when you're finished. It would take him a decade or so to want something more permanent, and even then it would be against his better instincts. He didn't need a house right now and he certainly didn't need a replica of mine. When we drove away, he hadn't even looked back at it.

I know all this better than he does. He probably imagines that whatever it is that's between him and Julie is more immediate. He may even think he's a bad lover or a bad person. I doubt he likes what he's thinking as the Connecticut countryside flies by and recedes behind us liked a welched promise. I'd asked if he minded driving, and he said why should he. Why indeed? It's his car.

"It's funny," he finally says when we hit I-91.

"Please, Russell," I beg him. "Don't tell me what's funny."

"Why not?"

"Because it won't be."

"What's funny is . . . I'm relieved."

"See what I mean?"

"No, seriously," he says. I suspect he doesn't know what serious means, though he's learning. "Ever since last night I've been trying to figure out some way to punish myself. Now I can leave the whole thing in your capable hands. You're about the most capable man I've ever known, Hank. I don't mind saying it's been a bitch competing with you."

I can't think what to say to this, but I have to admit, now that I've heard him out, that it *is* funny. "I hope you won't misconstrue my running you out of town as not liking you, Russell."

We both smile at that.

"Were you and Faye ever unhappy?" he asks.

"Together or separately?"

"Together."

"Sure."

He thinks about this for a minute. "I bet that's not true," he says. "I bet you're just saying it for one of your famous philosophical reasons, like happiness just isn't in the cards for human beings, the sort of thing guys like you say to college students in your late afternoon classes before you go home and spend a happy evening in front of the television."

There is a curious mixture of wisdom and naïveté in this observation, and it makes me even sadder to be putting Russell on a plane.

"Julie always says that's what she had in mind for us. To be as happy as you guys."

Once again I am aghast at how little my daughter knows me, at what a desert her imagination must be. What does she see when she looks at me? When I look at myself, the evidence is everywhere. I know now why she didn't come to see me at the hospital. It was the nature of my operation. It wasn't that she couldn't imagine me with cancer. She couldn't imagine me with a dick. That I am a man has somehow escaped her, which is why she doesn't think twice about bending over in front of me in her peasant blouse. And maybe it's even worse than that. If she has never thought of her father as a man, can she imagine herself as a woman?

Russell's car rides smoothly enough, but like most small Japanese models there is a low-level vibration that comes from being close to the earth and the buzzing engine. When the nausea I felt atop the lawn mower returns, I close my eyes and will it away, hoping that Russell will conclude I've fallen asleep.

"The good thing is I know now that I can't make her happy. That's what hitting her meant, I think. It was what I was thinking when I hit her. That I'd never make her happy. It pissed me off, because I always thought that was something I *could* do."

"You're very young, Russell," I tell him.

For some reason this observation also pisses him off and he looks over as if he's thinking about hitting *me*. "You can be one cold son of a bitch, you know that, Hank? You're just the kind of guy who'd kick a man out of his own house, take him to the airport in his own car, put him on a plane and figure he had a right to. The only reason I'm going along with this shit is because you look half dead. One little poke in the stones and I could leave you alongside the road for the undertaker."

"There," I say after a respectful moment of silence. "I guess you told me."

Bradley is crowded so we have to take the shuttle from a distant parking lot to the terminal. Then we walk a little and I begin to feel better again, waiting in line at the ticket counter, Russell behind me with his two suitcases.

When it's my turn, an earnest young woman wants to know how she may serve me. How do people keep such straight faces, I wonder. "Where can you go for two hundred dollars?" I ask her. "One way."

"Sir?"

I repeat my question.

"Lots of places. Boston. New York. Philadelphia . . ."

"Nothing west of the Mississippi?" Russell asks.

She shakes her pretty head. The farther you go, the more expensive it gets. Such is life, she seems to imply.

"Tough luck, Hank," Russell says.

"How about Pittsburgh?" I suggest, noticing that a flight's leaving in half an hour. I think of a woman I know who lives there, or did once. We met at a convention a dozen or so years into my marriage. My one infidelity. She had recently been divorced, and we made love more or less constantly for three days. Then she returned to Pittsburgh as I did to Faye, and I'd never heard from her again. For several years I stopped going to academic conventions, afraid that she would be there and I would prove faithless a critical second time. Lately, though I feel no real desire for her, she's been on my mind.

"Pittsburgh," Russell shrugs. "Why not."

There are only twenty-five minutes to departure, so we head for the gate.

"You can split if you like," Russell says. "You have my word I'll get on the plane."

In fact, I don't trust him. In his shoes, I would not get on the plane. Or maybe I'd get on and then off again, circling back to the departure lounge to watch whoever was seeing me off wave as the plane taxis down the runway. No, I intend to see him onto the plane, and then see it airborne. After that, if he wants to get off it's his business.

Blessedly, the gate is not far. I'm not looking forward to driving back home. I almost asked Faye to come with us, but that would've left Julie home alone. It occurs to me it's not just the drive I'm dreading.

"When you get there," I say, facing Russell, "let me know how to contact you. We'll need your signature to get you and Julie out from under the house."

"Sometimes I think it's the house that killed us," he admits without much conviction, as if it's one of a dozen equally plausible explanations he's considered in the last twenty-four hours.

"At least you don't have to go back to it," I say.

He gives a rueful laugh, then turns somber. "I wish you'd let me take the car," he says suddenly. "It's really not fair that I should end up in a strange city and not even have a way of looking for a job. I mean, I've been a shit and everything, but—"

In truth, I hadn't thought of this. Failures of imagination abound. And now that he's brought the unfairness of it to my attention, I know I can't put him on that plane.

"I swear to Christ," he says. "If you let me take my car, I'll go far away. Farther than Pittsburgh."

Right now, he seems about the most generous person I've ever known. After all, he doesn't need my permission. The keys I'm holding are his keys. They fit the ignition to his car. Only a combination of generosity and scalding guilt can account for the fact that he hasn't put up a fuss. By hitting Julie he has unmanned himself, losing everything but kindness. And I am suddenly sure he'll do as he says.

A voice comes over the intercom announcing that those needing assistance will be boarded first, then passengers traveling with small children. I hand Russell his keys.

"I didn't mean that about you being a cold son of a bitch, Hank," he says as we start back to the terminal.

"And you'd never poke me in the stones," I add, smiling.

At the sliding doors we shake hands, and I watch him lug his two suitcases across the huge parking lot. I don't feel too bad about him. Almost anyplace he ends up will be better than where he is now.

I'm left standing there holding an airline ticket to Pittsburgh that will need to be cashed in. Then I'll have to call Faye and admit to her what I've done. She will have to come collect me. It seems too much to ask—of either of us, so instead I head back to the gate. I arrive just in time to see the Pittsburgh flight airborne. "You're too late," says a young man in an official airline blazer.

"I guess so," I tell him. In fact there's no doubt about it. Odds are that she's no longer in Pittsburgh. She's probably married again by now, not that it matters, really. I only wanted to see her at some restaurant with half-moon booths where I might tell her about my surgery. For some reason I'm convinced that my brush with mortality would matter to her, and that I'd feel better after confessing to someone that I fear the nausea, that I consider it prophetic, a sign that some terrible malignancy remains. I remember her body and the way we made love, and I guess I was hoping that she would remember my body too. Maybe she would be afraid for me in the way I want someone to be afraid.

Back in the terminal I feed coins into the pay phone, dial and let it ring a dozen times before hanging up and trying Julie's number, which does the same thing. I'm too tired to be sure what this means. Probably Faye has given our daughter a sedative. Perhaps I have caught my wife in transit between houses. I wait a few minutes and try my house again, wondering if I've forgotten our number.

Whoever I'm dialing is not home. I go outside onto the terminal ramp and am about to ask a taxi driver how much it would cost to take me to Durham when Faye pulls up right in front of me, so I get in.

"I got to thinking about it," she says, "and realized you'd give him the car."

I just look at her, wondering if she might also have intuited that I just missed getting on a plane to Pittsburgh, that I had a lover fifteen long years ago who I want to tell things I can't tell my wife.

"You think I don't know you after thirty years?" she says, as if in answer to my unspoken question.

"Not intimately," I tell her.

"Hurry up and mend then," she says.

Night is coming and most of the trip back will be in the dark, but the car is warm and there will be no harm if I fall asleep. Faye knows how to get us home.

Joy Ride

We left early in the cold gray morning before I was entirely awake. My mother draped the clothes I was supposed to wear over a chair. My job was to get into them. Her job was to do everything else—pack the suitcases, throw them into the trunk of the car, write my father a note. When she came back to check on me and found me sitting at the edge of the bed, one shoe on, one shoe off, staring into space, she barked "Move!" so loudly that I jumped. And when even this failed to jump-start me, she kept saying, over and over, "Go go go go go go," which made me stare at her, stupid and a little frightened too. She came over to me then, getting down on her knees so we were face to face, and said, "Move, sweetie. We've got to move."

When I was finally dressed, I found her in the kitchen, trying to compose a note to my father, looking like she was in a one-shoe-on, one-shoe-off stage of composition.

When she became aware of me standing there, she scratched one big word in capital letters on the tablet and held it up proudly. GOODBYE, it said. "That just about sums up the whole deal," she said. "You got anything to add?" I shook my head. "You've still got sleep in your eyes, sweetie," she said, then worked her thumbs expertly in the corners of my eyes as I tried to back away. I was twelve and fully competent, in my view, to do this myself. "Okay," she said. "Let's go, before he comes home and finds us and the note both."

In the car she dropped a spiral notebook into my lap. When I opened it, I discovered it was a series of maps provided by the AAA Automobile Club. Each map covered a small area of roughly a hundred miles, and our route had been traced in yellow magic marker. When you turned the page, the next map picked up where the last left off, the yellow route highlighted across the new page. "You're the navigator," my mother said, turning the key in the ignition. I must have looked doubtful, because she added, "I can't do this all by myself, sweetie."

"Next time you see one of these," my mother said, indicating the harbor with her thumb, "it'll be on the other side of the country, a whole different ocean."

We lived in Camden, on the coast of Maine, and our plan, according to the AAA map guide, was to drive to southern California and, as my mother put it, to lose my father and lose him good.

"How come we're going through town?" it occurred to

me to ask. Doing so meant passing my father's hardware store. "What if he sees us?"

"What if he does?" she said. "It's not like he can see the suitcase in the trunk. He doesn't have X-ray vision. Half the time he can't see what's right in front of him." What was right in front of him, lately, was my mother, trying to pick a fight. Adjusting the rearview mirror so she could see herself, she ran her pinkie across her eyelid; her eyeliner was kind of heavy, and it made her eyes look Egyptian. There'd been other changes these last few months. She was growing her hair out, letting it go straight like the girls on TV. "As far as he's concerned, I'm taking you to school."

We were sitting at the town's only traffic light, and the hardware store was half a block up the street, a phalanx of bright red lawn mowers lined up in front. It was early April and there was still snow on the ground, but my father liked to encourage people to think spring. Studying the front of the store, I didn't have to look over at my mother to know she was looking at it too, as if daring my father to emerge. "Green," I said when the light changed. The car behind us honked before my mother could step on the gas, so she stayed right where she was, rolled down her window and stuck her arm out above the roof to offer a gesture I wasn't supposed to see. We sat right there until the light turned yellow and my mother punched us through just as it turned red, leaving the driver behind us to sit through another whole sequence. "Sit there, asshole," she said, smiling into the rearview mirror.

"You're swearing a lot this morning," I pointed out.

"Why shouldn't I?" she said. "It's a free country and I'm a free woman." When I didn't say anything, she continued. "It's not only a *free* country, it's a *big* one. Big enough for us to get lost in. We're bound for freedom, sweetie."

She was urging the car up the long hill that would lead us out of town and down along the coast to Portland. She had it floored, but the Ford seemed reluctant, and the engine was making a sound like there were marbles inside. "Downshift," I said.

She did and the car responded. Then she looked over at me. "You think I'm following *your* instructions all the way to California, you got another think coming, buddy boy," she said.

"I'm the navigator," I reminded her. "You can't do this without me."

But I could tell she'd lost interest in the conversation. At the top of the hill, I couldn't help turning around and taking one last look at the village below, at its three white church spires, the blue harbor, the Camden hills beyond.

"Peyton Place," my mother snorted, because our town was where that movie was filmed. "What a goddamn laugh."

Blowing town was my mother's idea, but right then it seemed an answer to my prayers, for I had fallen in with bad companions and was trying to impress them by acting crazier than they were. Craziness was something they understood and apparently admired, which was a revelation to me. Whenever I behaved like a lunatic, they clapped me on the back and congratulated me, and I liked their approval. These were the same young thugs, after all, who'd cornered me in the boys' room, back in the fall, two of them pinning me against the wall while the third peed on my chinos, turning them dark brown at the crotch and down both inseams. Then, for the rest of the morning, I was pointed out in the halls as a seventh grader who still wet his pants. To be admitted into their fraternity was more than just gratifying. These boys had taught me a deep human truth—that it was far better to be admired than peed upon.

Although not that much better, as I learned over the long winter months. My strategy had been to ingratiate myself further by performing small acts of insanity designed to capture their imaginations. One Monday during fourth period, having forgotten my lunch money, I dined exclusively on ketchup packets, consuming a whole tub of them for the entertainment of my lunch table. "You're one crazy little fuck, Dernbo," said the boy who had peed on my chinos, and the admiration I heard in his voice got me through the long, diuretic afternoon. To ensure that everyone understood that I was no flash in the pan, I repeated the performance the following week, this time with mustard, to even more disastrous intestinal consequence.

Gaining entrance to the dubious society proved disappointing, though of course I was unable to admit this even to myself. No group in my junior high school had a wilder reputation than my new friends, but as far as I could tell, it was largely unearned. They had let on—and of course it was believed—that during the summer they'd stolen a car and taken a joy ride down the coast to Old Orchard Beach where they'd drunk beer and met some high school girls who came across and they'd all spent the night on the beach.

This was exactly the kind of adventure I feared and longed for. I hadn't hung out with my new friends very long, however, before I began doubting that the episode ever happened. Either they'd lied or they only had the one joy ride in them. I was beginning to suspect that the most daring act they'd ever performed was peeing on my chinos back in October. By now, they seemed to look to me for inspiration, and increasingly I was responsible for the execution as well. I not only had to conceive of the smoke bomb in the tailpipe, but I also had to buy it with my own money and put it there. I was given to understand that it wasn't cowardice that infected my companions, but rather that they had records from their many run-ins with the cops. One more bust would land them in reform school, whereas I had years of credit stored up as a result of having been such a little pussy for so long. They were therefore determined that we should get on equal terms. Once we were all equally at risk, they'd start kicking ass again. Until then, we'd restrict ourselves to what we called small, random acts of senselessness—the lighted M-80 shoved through the mail slot, the burning bag of fresh dogshit on the WELCOME mat, sugar in the neighbor's gas tank.

But these were not what had me looking for an escape. The day before, on an impulse that frightened me into something like wakefulness, I had picked up a stone and thrown it, hard as I could, at a mangy dog that had just lifted its leg to pee on the tire of a parked car. My intention had been, I thought, to scare the animal off, to teach it caution, but I knew the moment I released it that the stone was too heavy, and I knew the moment I released it that it would neither miss the dog nor nick it on the flank. Suddenly aware of us, the animal put its hind leg back down and turned just in time to catch the stone right between the eyes, dropping without a sound. "Jesus, Dernbo," my companions said as one. By the time we ran, blood was oozing thickly through the fur.

"Let's haul ass," somebody advised. We were right there in the open on a quiet street, and it seemed impossible that what I'd done had not been witnessed. I stayed where I was, though, kneeling mesmerized beside the animal, amazed by the rise and fall of its narrow chest, its continued respiration. And after a few moments the dog jerked back to consciousness with a whimper, its rear legs twitching, and then it was on its feet, weakly licking my outstretched hand with the same look of stupid, affectionate confusion I'd seen on the face of old Mr. Conlan, our next-door neighbor, when he discovered that somebody had sugared his gas tank. It was that look I was hoping to leave behind as my mother and I climbed the hill that led out of town, reducing the whole village until it fit neatly into the round frame of the side-view mirror.

At Brunswick we got on the interstate and made a beeline for the New Hampshire border. To get across the state line suddenly seemed imperative to my mother, as if Maine had no extradition treaty with New Hampshire.

"You think he'll come after us?" I asked, a possibility that had been on my mind all morning.

"Your father?" she said with a snort.

I studied her. "What do you think he'll do?"

"Remarry," she said, checking the mirror again, which made me turn around and look too, even though I had no idea what to look for. We had the Ford, so if he was chasing us, it would be in a car we'd have no way of recognizing. When we crossed the Piscataqua Bridge, my mother still didn't relax, as I'd hoped she would, though she did say, as if talking to herself, "Okay, okay."

"You know the best thing about New Hampshire?" she said as we flew by the Portsmouth exits. "There's only about ten miles of it before you're in Massachusetts. In another fifteen minutes we'll be two complete states away from a certain hardware store owner of our acquaintance."

I squinted at her logic, knowing that my duty was to accept it. "We're not any farther away just because this part of New Hampshire's skinny," I pointed out, studying the appropriate page on the Triple A map.

"Don't be a smart-ass," she said. "You know what I mean."

"I don't," I assured her. It seemed important right then to disagree with her, perhaps because she was counting on me as an ally and I didn't want to be taken for granted. "I don't know what you mean."

I could tell, without having to look up from the map, that she was studying me. "I didn't have to bring you with me, you know," she finally said.

"All I said was—"

"I heard you," she assured me. "Loud and clear."

This was not a long conversation, but it was long enough if one of the speakers was driving a car and staring the other speaker down instead of keeping her eyes on the road.

A few minutes later we passed a sign welcoming us to the Commonwealth of Massachusetts. "There," she said. "See?"

Sure enough, Massachusetts was right where she said it would be, and we were now two complete states away from my father.

After an hour or so, we stopped for gas, and my mother had the attendant, who wasn't much older than I was, check the oil. I watched him. He opened the hood, stood there for several beats out of respect, then slammed it shut again.

"It's cheaper to pump our own," I said.

"That's true, sweetie, but we can't afford to break down." She'd taken the map book from me and was running her index finger along our route.

"Could you not call me that?" I said. I didn't mind it in private, just in social situations like the present one, when a teenager with a real job was hovering at the periphery of our conversation.

She didn't look up. "What should I call you—Conan?"

Which meant she'd found the comic books I'd hidden on the top shelf of my bedroom closet. "My name?" I suggested.

"All right, John Dern," she said. "Here's the plan.

We're getting off the interstate for a while. See some of this country, since we got to drive through the whole damn thing anyway."

Now I watched her. "I thought you said he wouldn't come after us."

"He won't," she assured me, watching the cars roar by up on the interstate. "He might report the car stolen, though. Technically it's his."

"Technically," I repeated.

"I think of it as half mine. Everything in marriage should be half and half, don't you think?"

"That makes *me* half his," I pointed out.

"Everything except you, sweetie," she said. "You hungry?" It was noon and we hadn't even eaten breakfast. "There's a Burger Doodle across the street if you're starving."

Burger Doodle was her name for any fast food outlet, and she held them all in contempt. "Personally," she said, "I'm too psyched for food. I'm gorging myself on freedom. I'm dining on air. Doesn't the air taste different today, sweetie?"

She was right. Where we were sitting, it tasted like diesel exhaust. When I offered no opinion, she started the car and put it in gear, then looked over at me. "Doesn't the air taste different today, *John Dern*?"

"I'm starved," I said, though I wasn't. The gasoline fumes were nauseating me. "We didn't even have breakfast."

She sighed, staring across the road at the golden arches.

She ordered me two cheeseburgers, fries and a large

Coke. For herself, just coffee, but before long she took a French fry, then another. When I began to slow down, midway through the second burger, she pointed a long, drooping fry at me and said, "I hope you're enjoying this. Because we're not Burger Doodling all the damn way to California."

We made it, that first night, to Waterbury, Connecticut. My mother's mood stayed buoyant the entire afternoon, as if she really was high on the pure oxygen of freedom. But she crashed shortly after we checked in and I think it was our room that did it. She'd opted for the smallest of several motels near the exit. "Independently owned and run," she explained. "They're always cleaner and cheaper and better than the chains." It might've been cheaper, but the room also was tiny and dingy, and bands of lines scrolled down the television screen on every channel. When I came out of the bathroom, I caught her counting our money at the end of one of the beds, and based on the look on her face I guessed that we'd spent more than she'd planned to that first day.

But there was a fancy-looking restaurant across the street, and she insisted on having dinner there to celebrate our first night of freedom. She got dressed up in high heels and a short skirt. Her eyes looked even more Egyptian. Twice she tried striking up a conversation with a man sitting alone at the next table reading a *Wall Street Journal*. "I've been in friendlier towns," she remarked to me, loud enough for him to overhear.

"This isn't a town," I said, twirling my spaghetti. "It's an exit."

At the next table the businessman curled his lips.

"What made me think you'd be good company on this trip?" my mother wondered aloud.

After we walked back across the intersection, my mother felt our car was "too conspicuous" so she moved it around back.

For some reason I awoke in the middle of the night thinking about the dog I'd stoned, the long odds of its turning right when I threw, how dazed and stupid the animal had been to conclude I was its friend. All of which scared me so bad I couldn't stay in bed. From the window you could see the off-ramp and hear the traffic rumbling down the highway. Despite the hour, cars were streaming into the bright Mobil station across from our motel. Despite my mother's assurance that my father wasn't the sort of man who'd follow us, it occurred to me, there in the rank darkness of our grungy motel room, that maybe she'd misjudged him. After all, neither of them seemed to suspect what kind of boy I was, their own son. And my father never would've guessed my mother was the sort of woman who'd just up and go, leaving him a one-word explanation. So maybe he was a different man than she— or either of us—knew. He could be closer than we imagined. Maybe this man we didn't know was right across the street, gassing up a borrowed car and getting ready to cruise the parking lots of all the motels. Maybe we were all in for some surprises.

. . .

Over the next few days we fell into a routine that was more leisurely and less contentious. We stopped whenever AAA or a highway billboard alerted us to some interesting attraction nearby. My particular interest was caves, and we made wide detours to visit a number of these, including a great one in New York State where you took an elevator down into the cavern and then got a boat ride. My mother was taken with places where you could climb up and look out over where you'd been and were heading toward, where she could feel the wind of freedom in her hair. We stopped at every scenic overlook, and she told me about a rotating restaurant at the top of some thirty-story building in California where we'd have a three-hour dinner and see everything there was to see. One afternoon in Ohio we saw the top half of a festively decorated hot-air balloon through the trees, and my mother immediately decided we had to take a ride in it. But the next exit was miles down the highway, and then we got lost trying to backtrack. When we finally found it, we discovered it wasn't a working hot-air balloon at all, just an advertising gimmick tied to a pole in the parking lot of a car dealership.

After that first day, we avoided Burger Doodles in favor of truck stops almost exclusively at lunchtime. "Truckers do this for a living," my mother explained. "They know all the best places." So we parked between semis and ate huge, open-faced turkey sandwiches and mashed potatoes or chicken-fried steak. I noticed that my mother enjoyed the way the men swiveled on their counter stools when we came in. "It's a good thing I've got you with me, sweetie," she said more than once as we studied our

menus, feeling the warm stares and hearing the soft mur-
muring of road-weary men her age and older, and I
thought there was just a shade of regret in her voice. Still,
the fact that I *was* there made me feel tough and important, like a man who maybe could protect a woman, not
just torment dogs and old people.

Nights we splurged, as my mother put it, at the nicest
restaurants we could find in the vicinity of the motel.
Often we'd have the place to ourselves, our entrance
interrupting some intimate conversation between the
cocktail waitress and the bartender. When there was no
one interesting to look at, we'd haul out the AAA book
and search the maps for attractions. "There isn't much
real life this close to the highway," my mother observed
sadly, checking her white lipstick, another new touch, in
the mirror of her compact. "The good stuff's all hidden
away, where only the locals can find it."

With each passing day we worried less about being
pulled over for driving a stolen car. We were paying for
everything in cash, so as not to leave a trail, and my
mother chortled each afternoon when we got off the
highway. About the only precaution we still took was
to park around back of the motel at night, usually in
the darkest corner. Which is how—in Joplin, Missouri,
at a Holiday Inn supposedly owned by Mickey Mantle—
the Ford was a sitting duck for vandals, who took what
the police said must've been a sledgehammer to the
windshield.

When we came out with our suitcases the next morning, the car was alive with glass. To make matters worse,
this was on a Sunday morning, which meant we had to

wait an extra day to make repairs. The motel manager pretended as best he could to be solicitous, and he did lend us a small whisk broom to sweep the broken glass off the seats. His mistake was to wonder out loud why we'd parked in the remotest corner of the huge lot. My mother had been looking for somebody to blame, and now she had her man. By the time she finished, she'd questioned his intelligence, his management skill, even his parentage. She'd also expressed her grave reservations about the Holiday Inn chain, the city of Joplin and the rest of Missouri, which she'd never admired in theory and liked still less in reality. Moreover, she doubted Mickey Mantle had ever stepped foot inside the place.

The manager was a small man, and it was clear he hadn't much experience in being dressed down by a woman as good-looking and angry and eastern as my mother. And she may well have been the first woman he'd ever seen wearing white lipstick. At any rate, he accepted her criticisms quite calmly, until the Mickey Mantle part. The Mick certainly did own this Holiday Inn, he begged to inform her. He came here all the time, and there were photographs in the lobby to prove it. Furthermore, it wasn't fair, in his opinion, to judge the whole state of Missouri on the basis of what happened one Saturday night in the furthest reaches of a single parking lot.

"That's another thing," my mother said, when the manager made the mistake of letting his voice drop. "What's this Missour-uh stuff? That's an 'i' at the end of the word, right?" By now we were back in the lobby, and my mother, spying a motel notepad on the desk, tore off a sheet, circled the word "Missouri" and underlined the end of it three times. How, she wanted to know, could the letter "i" be reasonably pronounced "uh"?

"Madam," the little man pleaded, "what does this have to do with your automobile?"

My mother was ready for this. "It just goes to show that people who can't pronounce the name of the state they live in should never be given a public trust," she said, and then told him we'd need a room for the night and that she expected it to be free of charge. Informed that a large convention of Baptists had booked the entire inn, and had already begun to arrive, she said, "Well, *un*-book it, Missour-uh, unless you want your snake handlers treated to some words they've never heard before, right here in the damn lobby."

So we returned to the same room we'd had the night before, where my mother crashed, as she often did after an outburst. "Watch some TV, sweetie," she told me, and within ten minutes she was fiercely asleep, her face clenched tight, her teeth grinding audibly. She didn't wake up until afternoon, and even then she was groggy and lethargic. I was sitting at the window, looking out into the parking lot. Our car, minus its windshield, was barely visible through the torrential rain that had been pounding down for half an hour. All the anger that had animated her that morning had now leaked away, replaced by something akin to grief.

"Why?" she said, looking out the window over my shoulder. Nothing had been stolen from our car, and that's what was troubling her, that this had been a purely malicious act. "What sort of person would do such a thing?" She seemed to have no idea she was sharing a room with a person who just might be able to explain it to her. After a minute she closed the drapes and turned the TV back on. Then she found some hotel stationery and started doing some calculations. Finally, she wadded these up and tossed them in the wastebasket. "What's all this going to cost?" she wondered, her eyes brimming.

By the time we went to dinner, her spirits were, if anything even lower. She'd showered and put on a normal-length skirt and neither eye makeup nor lipstick. The dining room was full of Baptists and every time we heard the word "Missouri," it was pronounced exactly as the manager had said it.

My mother sighed and contemplated her menu as if it were printed in a foreign language. "We've died and gone to hell, sweetie," she said in the voice she used for not-strictly-private observations.

That night, once I was acting like I'd fallen asleep, my mother slipped out. She was gone only a few minutes, just long enough, it later occurred to me, to make a phone call.

Unfortunately, the next couple days provided considerable evidence to support my mother's theory that we'd died and gone to hell. As we came down out of the green hills of eastern Oklahoma, what shimmered below was a truly hellish landscape—flat and dry and empty, as large as the ocean off the Maine coast, but brown. Suddenly the temperature was in the nineties, and our rain-soaked upholstery smelled musty. We didn't have air-conditioning, so we rolled down the windows and let the desert air thunder in around us like so many angry demons. The noise made impossible the conversation we'd lacked the heart for since Joplin, and the turbulence turned my mother's hair into a rat's nest of tangles. She didn't try to make out like it was the wind of freedom, either. She still wasn't wearing makeup.

As far as my mother was concerned, Oklahoma had even less to recommend it than Missouri. In fact, its single virtue seemed to be that its inhabitants didn't offer an unusual pronunciation. I tried my best to raise my mother's spirits, but she stared straight ahead at the empty landscape with palpable loathing. What had happened in Missouri seemed to have made her a fatalist, and now she seemed incapable of even fear, her most dependable highway emotion. Since Maine every time we were passed on the highway by a semi and felt the sensation of being vacuumed beneath its huge wheels, she tensed, bracing for the imagined impact. No more. She seemed not even to notice the big trucks as they roared past, blaring air horns at us, some of them. Her lack of concern was spooky, because I couldn't tell whether the miles had taught her that there was less danger than she feared, or whether the vandals of Joplin had demonstrated how vulnerable we were, despite all her care and planning.

We made fewer stops now because there was next to nothing, according to my mother, worth stopping for, though she did take grim satisfaction from paying a dollar to a toothless old man in Texas for the privilege of peering down a shallow, bowl-shaped well at a dense knot of lethargic, dusty rattlesnakes. However dispiriting, though, the snakes weren't our biggest problem as we blew like a hot wind through the panhandle. The glass was, and had been for days. Naturally, we'd done the best we could with the tiny slivers of broken glass that had rained throughout the car's interior. The company that replaced the windshield had vacuumed—once to their own satisfaction, and then again to my mother's—but the glass had worked itself deep into the seams and creases of the cloth seats, until we coaxed them out with our tender flesh. The microscopic shards insinuated their way into our haunches and thighs and behind our knees, registering first as mild discomfort, a squirming and scratching inability to get settled. Only later, starting the first night out of Joplin, did we realize what was happening. My mother was in the shower, and I heard her yelp as the hot, soapy water bit like gasoline into the scores of tiny cuts. Between us, we went through a whole box of Band-Aids that night.

"I don't know what to say, sweetie," my mother admitted when she finally switched off the lamps. "We're losing blood."

"Actually, it's a lot like being married," she explained days later as we neared the New Mexico state line, referring to the multitude of nicks that still had us squirming in the front seat of the Ford. "You don't quite know whether to shit or go blind."

The vulgarity made me look over at her hopefully, because it meant her spirits were on the mend. My mother enjoyed swearing, but it required effort and imagination;

so, when she was depressed or exhausted, her speech became timid and mild.

"Your father's not a bad man," she continued, broaching the subject we'd been avoiding for about two thousand miles and which had me pretty puzzled. I mean, I knew my father wasn't a bad man. He'd never been bad to me, and I'd never witnessed him being bad to her, but her desire to flee did imply there was something wrong with him.

"It's just that living with him—being *married* to him—is like being covered with these little cuts all the time. There's no big gash you can show anybody, nothing they'd believe would really hurt. But these damn little nicks, they suck the blood right out of you."

The desert rolled by as my mother's hair danced in the blowing air.

"I mean, *really*," she said after we'd gone a good ten miles, each of us pondering the man we'd fled. "Is that goddamn washer necessary?"

This was one of my father's quirky habits, manipulating a ring washer on the tip of his tongue as if it were a Life Saver candy. I have to admit, it could be a little unnerving, the first time you witnessed it. At the hardware store, his advice was sought on a great many projects, and my father was a thorough thinker who approached each new problem as if it were his own. He'd listen quietly, nodding at every complication or detail, and then he'd go into a pensive trance as he worked through various solutions, leaving his customer to his own leisurely contemplation. Sometimes he wouldn't say anything for a minute or two, his jaw working thoughtfully, and when his mouth finally opened it would not be to speak, but rather to reveal the silver washer on the tip of his tongue—as if the customer were being invited to reach out and take it, or my father were producing the very part needed to complete the job. Thus he gave the impression of being a man full of nuts and bolts.

Since this little trick might suggest an intellectual sluggishness, I feel compelled to point out that he was neither stupid nor without a sense of humor, nor unaware that some of his quirks drove my mother crazy. He knew that having a metal washer in *his* mouth made *her* teeth hurt, and so when a playful mood stole upon him, as it sometimes did, he'd attempt to joke her out of what he considered an unreasonable aversion. When he'd driven her to distraction, he sometimes liked to take her in his arms, whisper something sweet in her ear, bend down to kiss her and then, just before the kiss was to be delivered, show her the washer on the tip of his tongue.

The washer was not my father's only annoying habit. He ruined various games by losing sight of their objectives and obsessing over minutiae. Playing Scrabble, for instance, he wasn't content to consult one dictionary when challenging a word of my mother's, but would refer to as many as he could locate, getting sidetracked whenever he ran across an unrelated word that interested him. "Here's something," he'd say, furrowing his brow, while the other players at the table stared at him in quiet disbelief until my mother yanked the dictionary from his hand and hissed at him, "Play, goddamn it." Delighted, my father would grin and remark that even after all these years of marriage, he could still get her goat.

Much as I loved him, he was beginning to get my goat too. He liked to help me with school projects, rightly convinced that I was careless and missed things. Mostly, I wanted to be done, so when I got a glimpse of the finish line, I bolted for it; whereas my father loved to linger among the facts and pore over the library books I brought home. "Now *here's* something," he'd say again and again, though it was seldom a relevant something. Whenever he helped me, in fact, my grades suffered from his need for inclusion. Two-page reports weighed in at a bloated nine pages, and longer papers swelled to near monograph length. Then he'd go to school to argue the grades my teachers gave me, again losing sight of his objective by revealing that the work was more his than mine. "Slow and steady wins the race," he always assured me, a remark that never failed to elicit a sarcastic retort from my mother. "Lenny, you just *think* you won. All the other contestants finished long ago and went home."

"Your father lacks a sense of . . ." she explained to me now, as we rolled into the outskirts of Tucumcari, New Mexico. "Sense," she finally said. "He lacks a sense of sense."

Explaining my father's character deficiencies really cheered my mother up. By then it was early afternoon, and we'd planned to drive on through to Flagstaff, but Tucumcari seemed to be having a festival of some sort. A banner stretching across the highway announced "Cowboy Days," and the streets were full of men in cowboy hats and boots and jeans and shirts with metal snaps instead of buttons. A country western band was set up under an awning nearby, and some people were dancing in the hot sun.

"This is more like it," my mother said immediately, pulling into a motel that had a sparkling swimming pool and a sign out front in the form of a twenty-foot-tall cowboy boot. She pointed up at it as we pulled our suitcases out of the trunk. "That's what your father doesn't have the sense to pour piss out of."

I frowned. All this talk about my father had made me lonesome for him. I'd have given a lot to see him standing there, grinning at me, working his silly washer on the tip of his tongue.

"That's western humor," my mother explained. She'd been west once before, years earlier, after her parents had sold their house in Maine and moved to Phoenix, where they lived in a trailer park with a big swimming pool and lots of other retirees from cold climates. "Your father don't have the sense to pour piss out of a boot. Try saying it."

I didn't want to try it, and I said so.

"Sure you do," she said, and it was clear to me that we were going to stand there holding our suitcases in the blazing sun until I played along.

"Dad doesn't have enough sense to pour piss out of a boot," I said.

She contemplated my sentence. "Not 'doesn't have,'" she said. "We're in the West now. There's no such thing as grammar. It's 'He don't have enough sense to pour piss out of a boot.' Try again."

Once I'd said it to her satisfaction, we lugged our suitcases into the lobby, where she confronted a man in a cowboy hat at the desk. "I sure hope you ain't full up," she said. "We just come all the way from Missour-uh."

Walking down the hall to our room, she chortled. This was one of the best moods ever.

We spent the afternoon poolside, my mother in a new bathing suit, the only two-piece I'd ever seen her wear. At first we had the deck area to ourselves, but by midafternoon we had company and by four-thirty every chair was occupied, even the ones that didn't fold down. The pool had a diving board that pretty much guaranteed my happiness. I spent the afternoon showing off, doing flips, cannonballs, jackknives and what I termed crazy dives, which were mostly a matter of making grotesque faces before I hit the water. Still, at the edge of my exhilaration was a remnant of my loneliness, and this afternoon reminded me of another the summer before when we'd visited friends of my mother's who lived in Virginia and had a swimming pool of their own. My father fancied himself a diver, but that was because he couldn't see himself. The rest of us could, and he had my mother and her friends in stitches. The upper half of his body worked fine, but every time he entered the water, his legs formed a wide V. Informed that his feet were not together, as he imagined them to be, he kept trying, yet each time the V got even wider. He'd emerge, beaming, and say, "Better, right?" sending the rest of us into convulsions. "I could *feel* my ankles together that time," he insisted.

"Then how come we saw them flying apart?" my mother said, still laughing.

He appealed to me, the only one of the party, he seemed to imply, that he could trust. "What do *you* say? Together or apart?"

Now, in Tucumcari, I wished I'd lied. I could tell he hated the idea of looking ridiculous. But I'd told the truth, and so, despite my daredevil excitement here in New Mexico, I worried that I, too, was a ridiculous sight, and that perhaps I might grow up to be a man like my father.

As the deck area filled up, I could see that my mother, who seemed to possess every ounce of grace allotted to our family, was getting looks from men who found excuses to go the long way around the pool, past her chaise longue. She was wearing dark glasses and reading a magazine, but I knew she noticed them as well, and I knew how much it pleased her. Finally I quit the diving board to go over and join her, imagining that this was what my father would want me to do.

She must've had a similar thought, because when I plopped myself down beside her, she looked up and said, "Hi, sweetie. You come over here to protect me?"

"I'm tired of diving," I said.

"I guess this suit's cut too low," she said after another man strolled by with a long look. She demonstrated with her index finger what she meant. "I didn't realize until I put it on." This sounded insincere even to me.

Later, as we were gathering up our things to return to our room, the same man came back. He was tall and might have been considered handsome, but his legs and torso were bizarrely pale, in stark contrast to his face, neck and arms. Talk about ridiculous men, I thought.

"Well, I just got to ask, darlin'," he said to my mother. "What's with all the Band-Aids?"

We were both dotted with small circular Band-Aids on our legs and lower backs, though most of mine had come off in the pool. To my surprise, my mother told him the whole story about the windshield. I thought she made it longer than it had to be, and funnier than she'd thought at the time.

"It's a crazy old world, that's for sure," the man agreed. "But a good-lookin' woman like you shouldn't be traveling alone."

"I'm not alone," my mother said, which I took to be a reference to me. Apparently the man did too, because he looked at me then for the first time, and something about the way he sized me up made me feel like he wasn't standing corrected.

Our room opened onto the pool area, and when we'd crossed the hot cement and let ourselves in, I noticed, closing the door behind us, that the man was still watching us from across the patio.

The restaurant we went to that night was decorated with wagon wheels and leather saddles and harnesses. The waitresses and the cooks, who grilled steaks over an open-pit barbecue, all wore neckerchiefs and checked shirts that looked like they'd been made out of tablecloths. You could choose the size of your steak and how you wanted it cooked, but then you were through choosing. All the steaks came with baked potatoes and beans and garlicky toast.

A little sign on every table explained that the biggest of the steaks, a T-bone called the Monster, was free if you could eat it all. And this was what the huge man in the booth next to ours had ordered. It was brought to his table with a great flourish of bells, on a platter about the size of the one my mother used for the Thanksgiving turkey. About two inches thick, the steak barely fit. Having cavorted in the pool all afternoon, I was famished, unable to imagine a steak I couldn't eat. Yet here it was. One look convinced me. The big man seemed undaunted, though, and when the waitress set a little clock on the table and set it for half an hour, the man wordlessly dug in, sawing methodically, until the platter was a pool of blood, eating as if there were no particular hurry. Considering his task, I thought he had excellent table manners.

"Don't stare, sweetie," my mother whispered, but everyone else was, and pretty soon she was staring too. Paying no attention, the man devoured half of his T-bone in the first ten minutes, took a sip of water, consulted the clock and slowed down.

At this juncture, a waitress brought my mother a cocktail she hadn't ordered, then pointed across the room at the man who'd spoken to us that afternoon by the pool. He raised his glass in a silent toast, and my mother raised hers. "Hold up your Coke, sweetie," she told me. "Be polite."

I didn't, though. He hadn't bought me my Coke, and I didn't feel like being friendly. Besides, I was suddenly sure he had followed us to the restaurant.

At the next table the big man was eating more slowly now, and the little clock seemed to be ticking away faster. He cut the steak into small pieces and chewed them thoughtfully, beads of sweat glistening on his forehead and upper lip. With only five minutes left on the clock, he still had about a quarter of the steak to go; maybe another pound and a half. People at nearby tables began shaking their heads. He was a goner, you could tell.

But then he mopped his brow with his napkin and dug in again at nearly the same pace he'd started with, as if he had two stomachs, like a camel, and he'd just engaged the second. He didn't panic. The large pieces of bloody beef just entered his mouth and disappeared. The last bite went in with ten seconds left on the clock, and by the time the buzzer went off, he'd balanced his knife and fork on the edge of the plate and pushed it away, brushing off his hands with the satisfied air of a man who'd just finished a laborious but not especially complex task. A cheer went up when the waiter confirmed that the big T-bone had indeed been finished within the allotted time, and thus the man's dinner was on the house. When the applause died down, he looked over—we were still staring, I'm afraid—and said, "How do you do. I'm Clarence."

It hadn't occurred to either of us that a man who could eat a steak that big would be capable of speech. My mother was first to answer. "That's some appetite you've got there, Clarence."

He seemed willing to take this as a compliment, though he was not at all boastful. "I do this here about once a month," he explained. "It's good for business, and the owner is a friend of mine."

"Giving away five pounds of free steak is good for business?" my mother said.

"You bet," Clarence explained. "When people see it can be done, they want to try."

Right then, on cue, there was another flourish of bells as one of the massive T-bones was delivered to a man several tables away.

"They'll sell another four or five of those tonight and not one of 'em will be free. Plus everybody has such a good time watching that they'll tell the story to everyone from California to Maine."

"We're from Maine," I offered.

"Long way from home," Clarence observed. "You didn't come that far just to watch me eat a steak, I hope."

My mother and I introduced ourselves then, Clarence shaking hands with me first, then my mother. "Nice to meet you, pretty lady," he said.

"And I'm Bill," said the man from the pool, who'd materialized just then at my elbow. He was wearing tight blue jeans, and his cowboy boots, with ornate stitching and pointed toes, reminded me of the motel's neon sign. My mother introduced the two of us, then added, "And this is Clarence."

Bill did not deign to look at Clarence or me. "Me and Clarence go way back—don't we, Clarence?"

"We sure do, friend," he said, though it didn't seem to me that Bill was acting very friendly.

Still looking at my mother, Bill said, "You get enough to eat tonight, big fella, or are you still hungry?"

"I'm contemplating dessert, Bill. Dessert and some soothing conversation with my new friends here. They came about two thousand miles to watch me have my dinner." He grinned at me when he said this, and winked as if to suggest that we both knew all there was to know about this character and weren't all that impressed. "You could pull up a chair and join us, Bill. Take a load off."

Bill was standing there rather awkwardly, in fact. There was plenty of room in Clarence's booth, but Bill seemed to be waiting for an invitation to slide into ours. I couldn't tell if my mother hadn't asked him to because she didn't want him to feel that familiar, or because she hadn't extended any such invitation to Clarence, who wouldn't have fit.

"No," Bill said. "I just come over to see if this lady would dance one with me. That is, if she's up to it with all them injuries." He smiled then, and my mother must have liked it better than I did because she said she would, provided Clarence didn't mind keeping me company for a minute. Clarence agreed as if he'd been hoping to anyway, so Bill and my mother disappeared through a wide doorway into a large back room where a band had begun to play.

"What injuries?" Clarence wanted to know, sliding into my mother's side of the booth. So I gave my version of the story, which—like my mother's that afternoon at the pool—was almost funny, not the depressing development it really was but just one of those crazy things that happen to you on the road. I even made up a few details, since Clarence seemed to be getting a kick out of it. It took two songs for me to finish, and then our check came. Clarence paid it, on the spot, in cash, explaining that his own meal had been free and it was the least he could do for such hard-luck pioneers. "They got tables in the next room," he said, getting slowly to his feet. "Let's go make sure that rascal Bill isn't pestering your mother."

He wasn't. They were still dancing, or attempting to. Bill was trying to teach my mother the step everybody else was doing, a task made more difficult by the fact that he himself seemed not to have mastered it. He danced stiffly, as if his lower body, between his tight jeans and his cowboy boots, did not have the necessary range of motion. When the song ended, they came over to the table where we were sitting. My mother, who loved to dance and could never convince my father to take her, was flushed with excitement.

"Anyhow, that's the two-step," Bill was saying. "It takes a little getting used to, I guess." Then he pulled up two chairs. "You still here, Clarence?"

"Yes, but I'm thinking of taking my leave," he replied. "Though I might just ask John's mother to dance one with me before I go. I *do* enjoy mild exercise after a meal, don't you know."

"I'd be honored, Clarence," my mother said. "I was just getting the hang of the damn thing."

Bill sat down opposite me then. His face seemed pretty sweaty, and he watched my mother and Clarence on the dance floor without bothering to conceal his disgust. Clarence, it turned out, was a wonderful dancer, light and graceful on his feet, and he guided my mother around the dance floor among the other couples as if he had radar. With this huge man at her side, everyone in the room seemed to be watching her, as if what she was doing was as remarkable in its way as what Clarence had done with that Monster steak. And when they executed a complicated move, separated and came back together again in perfect time, my mother threw back her head and howled with delight.

The only person in the room not sharing her buoyant spirits was Bill, who I realized was now watching only Clarence. "Good," he said, getting up from the table with his empty beer bottle. "*Have* a heart attack, you fat fuck."

After the next dance, Clarence and my mother came back to the table just as Bill returned from the bar with another bottle of beer. Nothing for my mother this time, and nothing, of course, for me.

"You-all have a safe trip now," Clarence was saying, and again he winked at me. "I hope you've seen the last of your troubles. Keep your eyes peeled for coyotes and you'll be fine," he added, then extended his hand to Bill. "Always a thrill, William."

When Bill just looked away, Clarence refused to take offense, apparently content to shake hands with my mother and me. When he disappeared into the men's room, my mother turned to Bill and said, "That was rude."

He had a toothpick in his mouth that he was rotating thoughtfully, and this would've reminded me of my father and his metal washer except that Bill was clearly turning over a mean, ugly thought. "Well, Clarence is a pervert," he said, bringing my mother up short. "I wouldn't want him hanging around any kid of mine, but maybe that's just me."

"I don't believe you," my mother said, but the glance she threw me suggested a frightened confusion.

"Okay," Bill said, friendly again. "Suit yourself."

"I intend to," my mother said, and then, to me, "Let's go, sweetie."

"Let's part friends, anyhow," Bill suggested. "Dance one more with me, okay? Sweetie here can wait through one dance, can't you, sweetie?"

When my mother looked at me, I could tell she didn't want to, but God help me, I nodded for her to go ahead, suddenly sick with rage that she was allowing this to happen. I could think of nothing more humiliating than to be called "sweetie" by a man like Bill, and to know he could get away with it and there wasn't a thing in the world I could do. I hadn't felt such self-loathing in months, since I'd sat alone in the boys' room at school after eating all those mustard packets.

It was a slow song that the band was playing, and on the dance floor Bill kept pulling my mother toward him as she kept pushing him away. I couldn't watch. I knew it was my job to march out onto the dance floor and rescue her, but I also knew that I was only a boy. Worse, I had a terrible feeling that it wouldn't have made any difference if I'd been ten years older. I was a coward at twelve, and a coward I would always be. My throat constricted with the knowledge of who I was and what.

"Let's *go*," my mother prodded me in the side, the dance suddenly, finally, over, her voice containing an even

greater urgency than that first morning of our journey—
now so impossibly long ago—when I sat sleepily on the
edge of my bed. "Move."

Outside in the parking lot, I pulled away from her and
darted between a car and a pickup truck, where in the
dark I fell to my knees and let my dinner rise. I don't know
how long it took to bring everything up from inside me,
to put it out there on the ground where I knelt like a sick
dog, stunned and weak. I don't know how many times my
mother whispered, "Hurry, John! You have to hurry!" It
was only after she stopped that I realized we were no
longer alone in the parking lot, that Bill had come up
behind her and was blocking the patch between the
parked vehicles. When I finally got to my feet, the rancid
taste of the vomit still on my tongue, he said, "Stay right
where you are, sweetie, while I have a word with your
mother."

He had her up against the car now with his back to the
restaurant, so he never saw Clarence strolling amiably
across the lot toward us, looking like a man who had it in
mind to help someone change a flat tire. But I saw him.
Hurry, Clarence, I pleaded silently. *Hurry!*

"So, here we are, Little Miss Cock Teaser," Bill was
saying to my mother.

"I'm going to scream," she warned him, but the fear in
her voice was terrible.

"Nah, don't do that," Bill said. "Just tell sweetie here
what kind of woman you are. Just so he knows."

Hurry, Clarence!

He turned to me then. "You know what a pussy is,
sweetie?" he said, then reached up under my mother's

skirt and grabbed her between the legs. She went up on her tiptoes and her mouth opened like she was going to scream, but there was no sound. She was looking past him, off into the dark desert beyond the parking lot, as if at some betrayal she could not name, whose existence she had not suspected.

"This here in my hand is pussy. Course you'll probably grow up liking the other, like your fat friend."

Bill didn't know Clarence was close enough to hear this but must've sensed something, because he turned just as Clarence arrived.

"You stay the fuck out of this, Clarence," Bill said, but he let go of my mother and she slumped back against the car, sliding right down to the ground, clutching herself, whimpering, her knees together, her ankles splayed out on the pavement, her skirt up around her waist.

"Come on out here where I can get my hands on you, Bill," Clarence said flatly. He was far too big to fit between the two vehicles.

To this day I have no idea why, but Bill did what he was told, stepping forward sullenly, like a kid, to receive his punishment. Clarence grabbed him by the throat, banged the back of his skull against the cab of the pickup, then lifted him by the seat of his trousers and tossed him into the bed of the truck, where he landed like a sack of potatoes and lay still.

"There," Clarence said, brushing off his hands the way he'd done when he'd finished his steak and pushed his plate away.

.   .   .

The next day, as we sped across the desert into Arizona, we surrendered a lot of pretense, my mother and I. So far we'd been taking turns buoying up each other's flagging spirits, but it was suddenly as if we were sharing the same pool of emotions and the water in that pool had gone cold. I couldn't think of anything to say to her that wasn't accusatory, and I had the distinct impression she was somehow disappointed in me. When the silence became insupportable, I took out the AAA map book and thumbed through its pages dully, noting Carlsbad Caverns, south of us, without interest. We flew past scenic vistas—lava beds and Indian reservations—without even slowing.

And I was not surprised when at Flagstaff my mother turned down the highway toward Phoenix, where my grandparents lived. It made me bitter to think that we'd never make it to California, that we were not bound for freedom and never had been. This whole trip was nothing more than a joy ride, like the one my junior high friends had taken, and now I could understand their reluctance to talk about it. No doubt it had been a shabby thing, devoid of glory.

And I could see how our own joy ride would conclude. My grandparents would be expecting us when we arrived, my mother having telephoned from Joplin. She'd make a show of rebellion, refusing to return to her life in Maine, insisting she was through with all that, including my father. But they would point out that we had no money, that California was a scary place to live, especially for a woman on her own. She wouldn't say, as she had to Bill, that she wasn't alone, because she knew she was now, if she hadn't known all along. A twelve-year-old boy could protect her only from people who meant her no harm in the first place. "What day is it?" it occurred to me to ask.

"What difference?" my mother said.

"Date, I meant."

She looked me over for a minute, blankly, then returned her attention to the road. So I did it myself, counting the days forward in my head, starting with the day we left Maine. If my count was correct, then yesterday had been my birthday. I wasn't a twelve-year-old boy. I was thirteen. But like my mother said. What difference?

All of this was long ago. More than twenty years now, and as I think back on our joy ride that spring, it seems far more remarkable than it did at the time, and what followed more remarkable still. My father did not come for us, as I'd imagined he would. He couldn't afford to close the hardware store for that long, and it was cheaper for us to sell the Ford and fly back. He met us at the airport in Bangor, proclaiming it was the most wonderful thing in the world that we were back, and he hadn't been himself even for a minute while we were gone. And that was that.

My mother was from then on a dutiful wife, at what cost to herself one can only guess, and I choose not to. When he was diagnosed with cancer, she nursed him faithfully through long months of chemotherapy and radiation, and when he died, her heart was broken. This, I've come to conclude, is what people mean when they refer to life as a great mystery.

After returning to Maine, my mother and I seldom

referred to our flight, and over the years she came to insist that it had been nothing more than a vacation. We'd gone to visit my grandparents. My father simply couldn't get away from the store. After he became ill, this fiction became especially necessary—even essential, as I learned only after his death when, still stunned by the loss, I tried to open the subject of our betrayal so many years before. Probably it was forgiveness I was after, but if so, I'd come to the wrong person, because I'd never seen my mother as angry as she was when I suggested we'd actually wanted to break free of him all those years ago, that we'd made fun of him halfway across the country. She seemed to have forgotten entirely all the conversations I'd over-heard during the days we spent at the trailer park in Phoenix, when she'd confessed to my grandparents that she'd fallen in love with a wild and beautiful man who, though he didn't love her the way she loved him, had made her understand that her marriage to my father was little more than slavery. She had a wonderful spirit, he'd told her. She deserved to be free.

My mother's staunch denials angered me, and I let her know it. "Don't tell me you don't remember the boot, Mom. How you made me say it until I got it right, that Dad didn't even have enough sense to pour piss out of a boot."

"No, John," she said. "I don't. But I'll tell you what I *do* remember. I remember that the reason for that trip was *you*. What I remember was the vicious little monster you were becoming." She proceeded to remind me about all sorts of things I had no idea she'd ever known: how I'd fallen in with a pack of hoodlums, how I'd stoned a helpless animal, how my father had to pay for the repairs on our neighbor's car, how—in short, if she hadn't got me out of Camden when she did, I'd have been arrested and put in reform school like the rest of my so-called friends.

It's not the purpose of this narrative to suggest what kind of man I've become. I will say this much, though. I was sent to Vietnam during the last hopeless year of that war, and there I learned that I wasn't the abject coward I felt destined to become starting that night in a New Mexico parking lot. Vietnam provided opportunities for every imaginable cruelty, and these I discovered were not in my true nature. Although it must be said that my mother does consider me cruel, harsh in my recollections. And when we argue about the past, there are times when she can almost convince me.

But the worst truths are contained in our many silences. Too often the past will cause our eyes to meet furtively, guiltily, as they did one afternoon during the last days of my father's illness, after he'd returned home from a chemotherapy treatment. "The worst thing about chemo," he said thoughtfully, in that painstaking manner he had when reporting on some discovery in a dictionary or encyclopedia, "is the metallic taste it leaves in your mouth." He said this without irony, and then the shiny silver washer appeared on the tip of his tongue.

Buoyancy

For some time they'd been sliding from lush green into sepia, summer into autumn. Everywhere there were downed trees, slender birches and lindens caught up on power lines, trunks chainsawed into cross sections and stacked on the roadside, broken limbs, piled up next to gray-shingled houses. Even trees that had survived the hurricane were damaged, their trunks stripped naked and pink under the early September sky. In the wake of their car, brittle leaves danced and twirled along the shoulder of the road like distant memories.

"Oh dear," said the professor's wife, her voice a rich mixture of sadness and disappointment. She'd been worrying the white, scarlike crease of skin on the third finger of her left hand.

At the wheel, her husband, Paul Snow, eyed her gravely but didn't say anything, waiting instead for her to elaborate, though he was not surprised when she didn't. June had always been given to small exclamations that she left dangling, incomplete, and her "Oh dear's" were usually the tip of some emotional iceberg. To keep from colliding with them head-on, Professor Snow acknowledged their existence, as he sensed he was supposed to, then navigated around them with care lest his wife reveal the full nine-tenths below the waterline. She'd done so only once, years before, when her litany of lifelong grievances and womanly disappointments had come out in an amazing torrent, beginning with rage against him, but ending in almost unbearable regret and sadness, from which, it now seemed, she had never fully recovered her old self. Their family physician had assured him that his wife's moods had stabilized, that she was right to wean herself off her medication and he needn't watch her so carefully anymore. Professor Snow had been relieved to hear this, though it seemed to him that June's equilibrium was fragile still and could collapse without apparent, immediate cause. It was, of course, the immediate cause he was always trying to locate, having no wish to revisit the remote or universal.

"What is it?" he said.

By way of response, his wife failed to entirely suppress a shiver.

"Perhaps if we opened the windows," he suggested, rolling his own down and turning off the air conditioner. When the warmer air outside began to swirl through the car, he realized that he himself had been cold for some time. "Is that better, June?"

"Yes," she said unconvincingly. "Much."

But with the warmer outside air came the rich odor of decaying leaves, and once more Snow felt the disorient-

ing approach of winter and shivered
thought his wife hadn't noticed, becau
straight ahead and took such a long ti
edly, "We've come too late, haven't we

her h
h

On the ferry, though, under a bright late summer sky, the breeze on the upper deck billowing their clothes, they both cheered up. Out on the open water there was, of course, no evidence of the recent hurricane, nor hint of autumn, much less of winter. Here, as the early September sun warmed their skin, the Snows compared notes on what they remembered, what they'd forgotten and what had changed in the nearly thirty years since their last visit to the island. "The main biggest difference," the professor remarked, "is that we now have enough money to stay at an inn." On that previous trip— poor as a young assistant professor and his new, even younger graduate-student wife could be—they'd rented the cheapest cottage they could find in Oak Bluffs and still had to leave three days early because they'd run out of money.

In truth, Snow thought he'd forgotten all the details of that visit until many came rushing back to him: the way the cars were loaded, bumper-to-bumper, into the dark belly of the ferry; the gulls that sailed effortlessly along the upper deck, patiently awaiting a handout; the coin-operated viewfinders still mounted on both the port and starboard railings, promising to bring into focus the place you were going to, as well as the one you'd left behind.

Halfway across, June pulled a pale yellow sweater over

ead so she could feel the sun on her arms, and her
sband felt his heart go into his throat—imagining for
an instant that she'd forgotten herself, that she intended
to sun herself in her brassiere there on the upper deck,
and instinctively he reached out to prevent her.

How foolish, he thought, remembering too late that
she'd pulled the sweater on over a blouse as they left the
house that morning. This of course meant that he'd also
momentarily forgotten exactly who she was, this woman,
his wife.

But fate was kind and offered him an opportunity to
save face. "I seem to be snagged," June said, her voice
muffled inside the sweater, its fabric having caught on a
button, and there, even as she spoke, was his helpful
hand, already extended, as if to suggest that he was capable of anticipating her every need.

When they arrived at the Captain Clement House, the
front entrance was locked, with an elegantly printed note
affixed to the inside of the glass: *Please Enter Through
Garden*. They went around back, passing through a trellised archway into a manicured green world miraculously
untouched by the storm. The giant oak on the terrace
outside had been stripped bare, but the garden, surrounded and protected on three sides, was unscathed.
And perhaps because several dozen varieties of perenni-
als were in defiant bloom, there were yellow bees everywhere. The Snows did not linger.

"I'm so glad you're here," said the small, trim woman
who greeted them inside, introducing herself as Mrs.

Childress, the owner. She was of difficult-to-read middle age, with a not-quite-British accent and dark circles under her eyes. "For the moment you have the inn to yourselves. I'm rather concerned about the Robbins party. They're sailing up from Newport and I was given to expect them several hours ago, but I'm sure they'll be docking presently." She gave an elegant, sweeping gesture in the direction of the garden, as if to suggest that the schooner in question might this very second be tying up just beyond the French doors. "We islanders are all prey to a certain foreboding these days," she confided to June as the professor signed the guest register. "A remnant of the storm, no doubt. I'm sure they'll arrive safely."

Snow agreed, remarking that nothing untoward ever happened to people from Newport who owned sailboats.

"Well, I don't know these particular people," Mrs. Childress said, as if to suggest that therefore she had no idea whether they might be susceptible to sudden squalls at sea, "but they were quite delighted to learn we'd have a distinguished professor of American history in our midst. I warn you in advance that we're all bracing for a weekend of scintillating conversation."

"Ah," said Snow, whose discipline in fact was literature, "I'm retired, I'm afraid."

Mrs. Childress blinked, seemingly confused.

"I no longer scintillate," he explained, "though of course I used to."

The woman clapped her hands appreciatively and turned to June. "Isn't he the droll one?"

She then showed the Snows to a room on the third floor, from which they had an excellent view of the town and, in the distance, the harbor. Once she left, Snow followed his wife out onto the balcony, where he was relieved to find her smiling.

Back home in Ithaca, they had made gentle fun of the language of the inn's brochure, in which "resplendent" appeared three times. But Snow had insisted it was perfect for them, suspecting that despite their easy mockery, June secretly had her heart set on just such a place as the Captain Clement precisely for its "meticulously preserved, graceful formalities," its "artful blending of American and English, eighteenth- and nineteenth-century antiques," its "finishing touches of crystal and porcelain appointments," its "romantic ambience and elegant grandeur."

And after all, it was thanks to him that their return to the island, so often discussed, had kept getting postponed for well over a decade. Twice they'd canceled their reservations to accommodate some academic conference—most recently just last Christmas when Snow let himself be talked into his least favorite conference so he could sit on the committee interviewing shortlist candidates for his own position. He should have known better, of course, though he never would've imagined his colleagues might hire, over his strenuous objections, a young fool whose academic specialty wasn't even literature at all, but rather, as he proudly proclaimed, "culture." In the interview he used all the latest critical jargon, and assured the puzzled committee that his research was strictly "cutting edge." A month later, when the boy visited the campus—he seemed no more than twenty, though his vita stated thirty—he'd shown no deference to the department's senior scholars and exhibited a smirking contempt for Snow's own books. That so many of the professor's colleagues remained so enthralled suggested to Snow that perhaps they secretly shared his dubious opinion of his life's work. This realization was so bitter that he'd behaved badly, wondering at the question-and-answer session following the young man's presentation (on "Gender Otherness and Othering") whether students could apply his courses toward their foreign-language requirement.

But the boy was hired and Snow retired, willingly enough when all was said and done. The young fool would get his. In no time he'd be a tenured, fully vested *old* fool, by which time Snow himself would be contentedly cold and dead. Until then, however, he had to face June, who certainly understood that with retirement Snow had no excuses left. The Captain Clement beckoned, and he assured her that they'd enjoy traversing "floorboards worn to a glowing patina by two centuries of perpetual footsteps."

The morning after their arrival, the Snows slept in and went down for a late breakfast in the small dining room. Already seated were the two couples they'd met the afternoon before at tea, the people whose arrival from Newport had been awaited so anxiously by Mrs. Childress. They had mingled rather uncomfortably for an hour or so, the gathering supervised by their host, who seemed intent on holding it together by sheer force of will and a tray of sticky pastries. Later, at a restaurant close by, when the Snows casually mentioned where they were staying, they'd learned something about the Childress woman's anxiety from a loose-talking bartender. The Childresses had bought the Captain Clement only three years before, evidently paying well over two million dollars. "You got any idea how many rooms you gotta rent to pay *that* back?" the bartender had asked, arching an eyebrow significantly. No sooner had they closed on the deal than the bottom fell out of the island's real estate market—not to mention their marriage—and now the woman was good and stuck. The hurricane ruining the last month of the summer season would be the final nail in her coffin. The bartender had explained all this confidently and without visible empathy.

Indeed, the Captain Clement had an air of abandonment, the Newport foursome being the only other guests. Major Robbins, who owned the yacht, was retired military, and Snow couldn't decide whether he was naturally loud or compensating for deafness. Having been misinformed about the professor's area of study, Robbins had quickly cornered him and announced that he himself was something of a Civil War buff, proceeding to regale Snow with the tactical details of some obscure battle. Snow, loath to offend, first feigned interest, then distraction and finally—when the major said, "Now here's where it gets complicated"—intellectual exhaustion. Robbins was not alone in appearing disappointed when the Snows made their excuses and escaped through the garden, the major's party watching their retreat with the weary expression of people who'd been promised, then cheated of, a lengthy reprieve.

This morning, at breakfast, Robbins's companions looked haggard, as though a single night's sleep had not been sufficient for them to face this new day, though the major himself looked fresh and ready for anything. All four were dressed in beach attire and Snow noted with relief that they had finished eating and were unlikely to invite the Snows to join them. June, who professed to have enjoyed their company, was veering sociably toward their table until Snow touched her elbow and guided her to a table on the other side of the dining room. "Try the Mexican eggs," Major Robbins bellowed.

"I will," Snow promised, holding June's chair for her, a gesture that seemed appropriate here at the Captain Clement.

Mrs. Childress, who had been in the kitchen, came out to greet them and to inquire how they'd slept. Snow had slept badly, but insisted otherwise.

"What a shame we can't offer you breakfast in the garden," the Childress woman said, sounding almost stricken. "But the bees have claimed it, I fear."

From where they sat, the Snows could see that the garden was indeed set up for dining, pristine white tables scattered among the potted plants and hedges. They could also see bees swarming beyond the French doors.

"Are they the price of such lovely flowers?" June wondered.

"Alas, no," Mrs. Childress said, her faintly British accent kicking in again. "It's the storm. The bees are disoriented, or so we're told. They think it's spring."

Major Robbins noisily pushed back his chair. "The beach!" he cried, as if commencing a dangerous amphibious assault, though his troops looked potentially mutinous. The major's wife, the first to venture outside, let out a whoop as the bees closed in and then she bolted for the white trellised arch, arms flying about her head, her companions close behind, also beating the air wildly.

The Snows' waitress was a pretty girl named Jennifer whose tan was dark and remarkably even, Snow noticed when she bent to pick up a fork she'd managed to knock to the floor. He wondered whether it was the girl's clumsiness or her immodesty, given the scoop-necked uniform that caused Mrs. Childress to roll her eyes at June before disappearing into the kitchen.

"South Shore has the best beaches," the girl explained in response to Snow's question about where they might spend the afternoon. "Really awesome bodysurfing."

As the girl said this, he thought he saw a trace of doubt flicker across her heretofore untroubled features, perhaps registering her realization that bodysurfing might not be what these particular guests had in mind.

"Oak Bluffs is nice too," she added hastily. "That's got a lagoon."

Another flicker of doubt—had she insulted them?—and a weak smile, as if to concede she wasn't the person to ask. She didn't know what older people did, or where they did it, or why.

Her plight was so touching that Snow decided to help

her off the hook. "Which is the beach with the cliffs?" he asked, suddenly recalling it from their previous trip.

"Gay Head, you mean?" the girl said, surprised. "That's clothing optional."

"Oh," June said with a wry smile. "Well *that's* out then."

"Right," the girl said sympathetically, though Snow couldn't tell if she was reluctant to shed her clothing in public now or if she was looking ahead thirty years. Actually, if they stayed right around the area where the trail joined the beach, they'd be fine. It was only farther down the beach, beneath the bluff, where the nudists gathered. They liked to cover their bodies with moist clay from the cliffs—"it's primo skin conditioner"—and then let it dry in the sun. "And don't worry about the name. Some people think it's a gay beach, but it's not," she concluded, as if she felt it her duty to allay their fears on this score at least. "They probably ought to call it something else."

"Perhaps they could call it Primo Beach," June said wryly when the girl stepped away.

While she was in the bathroom changing into the new bathing suit she'd bought on impulse the day before while they were waiting for the ferry, Snow called his old colleague, David Loudener, whom they'd planned to visit in Manhattan on their way back to Ithaca. David was one of very few people who knew the details of what had happened when June suffered her breakdown. In fact, he'd been with Snow when the police had called to say she'd been found at a nearby shopping mall, staring into the empty display window of a vacant store, and together they'd gathered her up and taken her home. Apparently, the only consequence of her brief disappearance was that she'd given her wedding ring to a stranger.

This was years ago, but "How's June doing?" was David's first question, and Snow imagined he heard concern, perhaps even fear, in his old friend's voice. Snow again was reminded of his suspicion at the time that David blamed him, at least in part, for what had befallen his wife. "You're going to have to be careful of her," he'd told Snow after she was released from the hospital, and something in his friend's voice suggested that he doubted that caring for June was a task he was suited for.

"We're both fine," Snow now said, aware that June was probably able to hear the conversation through the bathroom door. "Anxious to see you and Elaine." And once again he took down the complicated directions he'd need to follow into Manhattan.

"This is way too young, isn't it," June said when she emerged from the bathroom, modeling the new white swimsuit.

Snow couldn't tell whether this was true or if it was his wife's posture that proclaimed, almost defiantly, her determination to act her age. June was still trim—athletic-looking, in fact—but clearly she was not about to cut herself any slack. In a sunny mood when she'd gone into the bathroom, she now appeared discouraged and uncertain. "You look wonderful," he assured her. "Come here."

She ignored this invitation. "It's cut too high in the

leg," she said, tracing the line of the suit with her index fingers.

"It's the way they're wearing them," Snow said, though now that she'd drawn his attention to it, he saw what she meant.

"It's the way twenty-year-olds are wearing them," she said. "Twenty-year-olds with primo bodies."

"You look lovely, June," he said.

"You'd let me go out in public looking like a fool, wouldn't you," she said.

"Dear God."

"At least I had sense enough to buy this," she said, slipping a mesh cover-up over the suit.

As they drove up-island, the devastation of the hurricane became even more pronounced. Obviously, cleanup had been prioritized, and the less populated side of the island was still awaiting attention. Along the winding road, branches and other windblown debris still littered the roadway, though larger downed limbs had been dragged onto the shoulder. The air was thick with yellow bees, which pinged angrily off their windshield.

But further on the landscape opened up, rewarding them every quarter mile or so with a glimpse of blue ocean, until finally the road climbed and narrowed and there was blue sky and ocean on both sides. June's spirits seemed to lift as the car climbed the final stretch toward the lighthouse perched on a cliff. Halfway down the boardwalk path to the beach, they stopped so June could pull off the cotton cover-up, and she surrendered a grudging smile. "There," she said. "Are you happy now?"

"I *was* happy," he protested. "I *am* happy."

"Feel that breeze," she said.

By the time they got to the beach, Snow realized he was out of shape and allowed June to carry the beach chairs while he shouldered the bag that contained their towels and suntan lotion, his wallet, her purse. She didn't even point out that she'd cautioned him against taking these particular chairs—bulky and old-fashioned, with heavy wooden frames—instead of the lighter aluminum ones. These had looked flimsy and chintzy to Snow, who'd thought they should recline in good sturdy beach chairs and sleep in an elegant inn.

At the end of the boardwalk, the beach was relatively crowded with bathers, but by trekking a bit farther they could have a stretch of sand more or less to themselves. "By all means," June agreed. "In this suit I want to be as far away from people as I can get."

It looked to be about three hundred yards to the rocky point, with the red clay cliffs rising gently along the way. They'd gone not quite a third of the way when June dropped their chairs in the sand and said, "This is as far as I go, buddy boy. Look up and you'll see why."

Snow, more tired than he cared to admit, had been slogging through the sand with his head down. "What?" he said.

Further up the beach, directly beneath the tallest cliffs, was another smaller cluster of bathers, which caused him to wonder if there'd been a different path that led more directly down to the beach.

"Those people are naked," his wife said.

Snow squinted, salty perspiration stinging his eyes. "Are you certain?" While recognizably human, the figures down the beach were too far away to be, as his replacement might put it, "gender specific."

"You need glasses," June told him, setting up her chair.

He dropped their bag in the sand. "I need *binoculars.*"

Overheated, they went for a swim. The September water was still wonderfully warm, and Snow, who as a young man had loved to swim, dove into the surf and swam out beyond the breaking waves where he did a leisurely crawl before letting the surf bear him back in. June was not the sort of woman who plunged right into anything, much less the Atlantic, and he was not surprised to see that she was still feeling her way out. She had always been a graceful woman, and now, in her midfifties, still had a way of meeting the swells that seemed to him the very essence of womanhood. The waves never broke over her, never knocked her back. Rather, at the last moment, she rose with the water, right up to the crest, and then went gently down again. How long, he tried to recall, since they had made love?

Perhaps his wife was thinking the same thing, because as he swam toward her, her smile in greeting contained not a single reservation, though its cause may have been merely the joy of water, the thrill of buoyancy. "Oh, this is grand," she said, water beading in her hair and lashes. When they embraced, she whispered urgently into his ear, "I'm sorry I've been such a pill."

Such a pill. As Snow embraced his wife, it occurred to him that the last time she'd used this phrase, she'd been a young woman, and their love for each other had been so effortless that whatever had momentarily come between them could be effectively banished with this benign phrase. What it conveyed now was not just a sudden and powerful resurgence of affection and trust, but also promise that the difficulties of their marriage over the last decade might even now be swept aside by a mutual act of will. They could be their old, younger selves again. They would be in love.

Later, as they stood in the warm sand toweling themselves dry, June looked down at herself and said, "Thank heavens it's just us." The bathing suit that when dry had caused her so much anxiety proved, now that it was wet, somewhat less than opaque, and her nipples showed through clearly, as did the dark triangle of her pubic hair. And to Snow's surprise, she seemed less upset than she'd been when she emerged from their bathroom at the Captain Clement, insisting that the suit was too young, that she looked foolish.

"Let's move our chairs up under the bank," she suggested with a mischievous glint in her eye, a thing he hadn't witnessed in a long, long while.

"Why?"

But she was already carting a chair and the beach bag toward the bank. Tired, happy and suspicious, he folded up the remaining chair and followed. The tides had eroded the cliff irregularly, of course, and the spot where June set up her chair was semiprivate. Still, he was astonished when his wife peeled off her bathing suit and stood naked before him, this woman who for years had changed into her nightgown in the bathroom. "Well?" she said.

"Well what?"

"Let me know if we have company," June said, settling into her chair and putting on sunglasses. "Unless you're embarrassed, that is."

"Why should I be embarrassed?" he said, staring down at her.

"Good," she smiled, taking a book out of the bag.

Snow set up his chair next to hers, realizing that a challenge had been issued and there was nothing to do but answer it. When he dropped his bathing trunks, she looked at him critically over the rim of her sunglasses. "I *beg* your pardon," she said.

The night before, having returned from dinner only to discover that he'd neglected to pack a book, Snow had slipped into a pair of Bermuda shorts and a T-shirt and padded downstairs in his bare feet to the library where tea had been served that afternoon. What he found was discouraging, if not surprising. Many of the volumes were Reader's Digest Condensed Books, and as he scanned the shelves for something vaguely worth reading, he realized that there could be only one plausible explanation for such a bizarre collection: that the books had been purchased in bulk to provide the Captain Clement's "romantic ambience." Some were water-damaged, their brown, brittle pages stuck together, and others were upside down.

Perhaps because it was one of the latter, Snow did not immediately recognize his book on Emily Dickinson. He had to remove it from the shelf to be sure, but there he was, twenty years younger, staring up seriously from the dust jacket. How strange, he considered, to discover himself in such a place. How had he come to be here, inverted, next to the far likelier Thomas Costain? He examined the book curiously, including the endorsement on the inside flap: *With steadfast scholarship, Paul Snow penetrates the deepest secrets of one of literature's most private lives.*

This was precisely the sort of criticism, of course, that his young replacement had scoffed at. A twentieth-century male scholar "penetrating" the secrets of a nineteenth-century female poet? Such effrontery, according to the new thinking, would reveal only the prejudices and assumptions of the author's own culture and gender. How ironically vindicated, Snow thought ruefully, this champion of culture and gender would feel to learn that Snow's best work had been consigned to the "the gentler elegance of a bygone day," at an inn on its last legs. Instead of replacing the book on the shelf, he laid it flat on a table where Mrs. Childress would notice it in a week or two, and perhaps recognize her guest from the dust jacket photo.

Returning to their room with a newsmagazine, Snow paused at the foot of the stairs, rooted there by the muffled, distant sound of a woman weeping. Although he had left June engrossed in a book, his first thought was that this grief, although sudden and unannounced, must be hers, and so he remained where he was, paralyzed in the dark, until he realized that the sound was coming not from above, but rather from behind the door marked PRI-VATE. Indeed, June was safely asleep in their room, facing the window, its sheer curtains stirring in the warm autumn breeze. Still, though the grief he'd heard below was not his to share, it haunted him, and he awoke several times during the night to the sound of weeping carried upward along the ancient ducts and floor registers, and he lay in the dark for what seemed like hours, alert to the measured sound of June's breathing and guarding against the possibility that some deep sympathy with another woman's grief would reawaken her own. But she continued to sleep peacefully. Once she changed positions and murmured a word softly, and he noticed that she massaged her ring finger before rolling over again, but she did not wake and her sleep seemed untroubled. Since giving away her wedding ring, she'd refused to let him replace it, though he made up his mind to broach the subject again before they left the island.

Perhaps because he'd slept so fitfully, he now fell dead asleep on the beach, drawn downward by the rhythm of the waves. When he woke, it was to the realization that he'd been sleeping for quite some time. He vaguely remembered that just before he'd drifted off June had touched his arm gently and suggested he put on sunscreen, but there had been a cool breeze off the water, and he was enjoying the feeling of his skin tightening as it dried in the sun. His skin felt warm now, but he still felt no urgency about waking completely. How pleasant it was just to lie there with his eyes closed, thinking of June's warm embrace—her acceptance of him—in the waves, listening to the surf and the voices and laughter carrying all over the beach.

He opened one eye. When he'd fallen sleep, he and

June had been *alone*. But no longer. A few yards away a young woman had just released a Frisbee, and he followed its flight toward the water; a small dog leapt into the air, caught it in its mouth and trotted back. The girl was wearing a T-shirt and a tiny black bikini bottom, the smallest he'd ever seen. No, she was wearing *no* bikini bottom. At which point he remembered he'd fallen asleep naked himself, and sitting up straight, he saw that he still was. Also that June's beach chair was empty.

She'd gone for a walk, of course, or a swim. Except that he didn't see her in the water, and when he looked for the beach bag, he saw it was no longer sitting beside her chair. Surely she wouldn't have taken the bag if she'd just gone for a walk. And it was unlikely she would've taken a walk, now that their stretch of sand was populated, however sporadically, by naked people. The beach was still not crowded; the nudists, mostly young and in couples, had bivouacked at discreet distances. The only person who wasn't young was a gray-haired man with an enormous belly, standing at the water's edge and looking out to sea. Apparently he occupied a nearby blanket, and from this Snow was able to see in his mind's eye what must have happened. As the man, clothed, had come up the beach toward them, June would've looked up from her book. She was certain to have put her own suit back on by the time the first stranger appeared around their spot. She'd probably flashed the man a noncommittal smile, an acknowledgment of their similarities in age and attitudes about public nudity. Perhaps the man even smiled back as he disrobed. Lord, Snow thought.

Then an even worse scenario occurred to him. Perhaps

June, too, had fallen asleep under the seductive sun, only to awaken suddenly, as he himself had done, naked and surrounded by beautiful young bodies. He imagined her on the verge of tears, feeling humiliated and old, struggling awkwardly into the bathing suit, losing her balance in the sand, convinced that everyone was staring at her. Hastily, she'd have pulled on the mesh cover-up as well. But why hadn't she woken him up? Because she never did, not even when things were bleakest for her. She'd given him no sign the morning of her breakdown; she simply hadn't been there when he returned home. And while their physician, an old friend, had claimed that a relapse was highly unlikely, Snow also knew that to battle depression, you must first spot its early warning signals. But what if there weren't any?

Shading his eyes with his hands, Snow stood and gazed up the beach in the direction they'd come, half expecting to see his wife's fleeing form. In the glare, the sand stretched on forever.

Hastily drawing his bathing trunks back on, he told himself that the most important thing to do was to find her as quickly as possible. She was probably weeping quietly in their car up by the lighthouse. It *had* been June he'd heard weeping last night in the Captain Clement, he was suddenly, irrationally, certain.

The top of the lighthouse was just visible from where he stood, an impossibly long way off, it seemed to him, since he'd have to retrace his steps up the beach and locate the boardwalk that snaked leisurely up the cliffs. Again he noticed that at their rocky base, maybe a hundred yards down the beach, there was that other concen-

tration of bathers, and he resolved that there had to be
another trail to the summit. A shortcut. Steep, perhaps,
but more direct. Depending on how much of a head start
June had, he might be able to intercept her.

Regardless of which route he took, he would have to
leave the chairs. He hadn't managed to carry them all the
way here, so he certainly couldn't pack them up the side
of the cliff on the path those other bathers must have
used. Leave the chairs, he decided. He didn't want the
chairs. He wanted June. He thought about how, just a
short time ago, they had embraced in the waves, and
about his sudden optimism. Had he been foolish to think
that all could be made right between them? To imagine
their marriage was buoyant as water, their mistakes
weightless and inconsequential in the sudden swell of
affection?

And so he started down the beach, the hot sand giving
beneath his feet with every step. The rocky promontory
was farther away than it looked. Much. By the time he'd
gone fifty yards, the top of the lighthouse had disappeared, and the cliffs themselves loomed up above him,
high and jagged and steep. In some stretches the clay was
bright red, in others gray. From a distance these alternating striations appeared to be narrow ribbons, but in actu-
ality they were thirty yards wide. He kept an eye out for a
path, but every place that looked promising had a sign for-
bidding climbing on the fragile cliffs.

What had appeared to be a concentration of bathers
at the foot of the cliff turned out to be isolated groups of
privacy-seeking nudists. Despite this, Snow continued

down the narrowing beach, the bright blue ocean on his left, the cliffs looming ever higher on his right, the hot sun at his back. He'd forgotten what it was like to hurry through sand, and when his calf muscles began to throb, he slowed, fearing he wouldn't have enough strength left to climb the cliff when he finally found the path.

But within three hundred yards or so—his lower back pulsating, his breathing labored—he saw the error of his reasoning. At the promontory the beach turned north, and before him lay another stretch of sand as long as the one he'd just traversed, this one entirely devoid of people. Staring up at the cliffs, he realized there *was* no shortcut. The top of the lighthouse had come back into view, behind him now, and his heart plunged at the sight of it. How far he'd come! He'd be lucky to make it back to the beach chairs, much less to the boardwalk that led toward whatever remained of his marriage.

And what did remain? Even in his exhaustion Snow could clearly recall the litany of anguish and accusation that June had laid before him years ago in the hospital. By marrying her, he had stolen her own bright career, made her a dinner-party hostess to people who would've been her colleagues. Had he any idea how badly she'd wanted children? And did he realize that she knew, had known for years, about the long affair he'd had with one of his graduate students? When he told her that no words could express how ashamed he was, how bitterly he regretted this infidelity, June had said, with genuine rancor, that she was sorry to hear it, because she'd had an affair of her own that she didn't regret in the least. Snow had not believed this, concluding that she simply wanted to wound him; and later, when she asked him to forget everything she'd said, to write it off as menopause, he found to his surprise that he was able—no, eager—to.

It was almost out of reach now, he thought, staring up the beach and into the immediate future. There would be the drive back to the ridiculous Captain Clement and, a day later, the complicated journey to Manhattan, which seemed more confusing each time he visited, where he sometimes got lost and no longer possessed the knack of knowing where he and June would be safe. Then the return to Ithaca, a place far too familiar and claustrophobic ever to get lost in, no matter how much one might wish to.

As he started back, knees jellied and back throbbing, Snow discovered that even now he felt lost, despite knowing that all he had to do was retrace his steps. With the cliffs on one side and the sea on the other, there was no possibility of a wrong turn, but the sun was in his eyes now—doubly, it seemed, because of the glare off the water—and if he wasn't careful he'd walk right past the beach chairs in their secluded alcove. And how would he know when he'd arrived at the place where the boardwalk joined that beach? The huge beach was impossible to miss from the boardwalk, but the boardwalk might be virtually imperceptible among the dunes. He imagined himself marching doggedly, stupidly, up this beach forever.

Still, there was nothing to do but keep moving. Because of the blinding glare and the sting of sweat in his eyes, he sometimes didn't see the sunbathers until he was almost on top of them, and one startled young woman quickly rolled onto her stomach and glared at him angrily over her shoulder. When she nudged the sleeping boy next to her, Snow mumbled an apology and hurried on, staggering in the sand. How could he have been so foolish as to assume the existence of a second path? He plunged forward, blindly now, on the verge of panic. His sunburn—he suddenly was aware of it—was making him lightheaded. He was inhabiting a nightmare where everything was inverted: instead of discovering himself naked in a crowd of friendly, well-dressed strangers—wasn't this how such dreams usually worked?—here he was, an old man in baggy swimming trunks, adrift in a sea of angry, naked strangers. And what phantasm, dear God, was this, coming languidly but directly toward him down the beach?

He stopped, transfixed, certain he had lost his mind. Was it a young woman or a hag? Incredibly, she was both. Her skin, from head to toe, was a dry, cracking, lifeless gray. The figure resembled, frighteningly, a photographic negative. Its naked breasts were large and full, the dry seaweed between her legs the color of pale ash. Only her eyes were white until her smile—lewd, he thought—revealed rows of sharp, perfect white teeth.

"Dear God," he said, dropping heavily to his knees, far too exhausted even to try to flee.

Perhaps because the dry hand on his shoulder was both warm and gentle, he found the courage to look up at the gray skull, which was fearful still, though no longer grinning. Its expression seemed almost apprehensive, the last thing he would have expected, now that he'd recognized the figure.

Not now, he thought, pleading. He could feel his heart thudding dangerously in his chest. *Please, dear God, not now.*

The trip back down-island took almost an hour—an eternity, it seemed. If the world had finally righted itself, it was at his expense. Snow felt like a man with very little time left.

June, at the wheel, looked less old than shattered. She'd been able to explain her part in what had transpired in a few terrible, clipped sentences. When he'd awakened, she'd been swimming. The current had borne her down the beach, from where she'd seen him stand to look around for her. She'd waved, unsure whether he'd seen her or not when he pulled on his bathing trunks and set off walking, she'd assumed, to look at all the pretty naked girls. She'd felt self-conscious about her own nakedness at first, but the sensation had quickly vanished, replaced by an odd, pleasant sense of liberation. Before going into the water, she'd stuffed the beach bag under the chair he was sleeping in. He'd have seen it there if he'd looked.

Their arrival back at the Captain Clement had been the final humiliation. June had to lead him like a blind man under the trellised arch, and halfway to the French doors he'd slumped onto a wrought-iron bench, the garden path swimming before him. It was several minutes before he was able to stand. June had remained there

with him, though she refused to sit or speak, the two of
them in a dense cloud of bees, in full view of the library
where Mrs. Childress had gathered the Newport people
for tea.

Shortly afterward, June went out in search of first aid
cream, leaving him in their room at the top of the inn.
For the second time, they would be cutting short their
stay on the island, and Snow was certain his wife would
call David Loudener and cancel their visit to the city.
What excuse she would offer, he neither knew nor cared.
June had been gone only a few minutes when there
was a knock at the door, and Snow, who at the moment
couldn't think of a single person he wanted to see, was
rewarded for his misanthropy by the sight of the one person who in all the world he wanted to see least.

"We'll be checkin' out early," Major Robbins explained.
"I don't think we could take another night in this place,"
he said, glancing around the room contemptuously.
When it became clear that the professor hadn't gotten
this, he said, "You didn't hear that caterwauling last
night?"

Snow, even more confused, wondered how this half-
deaf major could possibly have heard June's grief.

"You're lucky you're up here on the third floor," the
man said, rolling his eyes. "I don't know what's wrong
with our hostess, but she bawled the night away. The wife
and I are right over her bedroom."

"The poor woman," Snow said.

"Well, yeah. Sure, but Christ Almighty."

"Would you like to come in? My wife just—"

"Yeah, I saw her go," Robbins interrupted. "I just wanted to make sure you were okay. That's some sunburn you got."

"I'm feeling better now," Snow said, though in truth he was still feverish, and when he touched the tender skin along his forearm, his fingerprint shone white as a scar.

"I'm glad," Major Robbins smiled skeptically. "Anyway, I came up to tell you I saw that book of yours. Down in the library? It looked interesting."

"I'm told it's passé," Snow said.

The major dismissed this with a wave. "I always thought it would be really satisfying to write a book. Leave something behind for people to remember you by. Like history, almost."

The two men shook hands then, and Snow closed the door and listened to the major lumber down the two flights of stairs, a kinder man than he'd imagined. Instead of lying back down on the bed and risking a feverish sleep, he went over to the window and looked down in time to see the Robbins foursome dart through the trellised arch and head down toward the harbor, carrying their canvas duffel bags. They were dressed in shorts and white cotton sweaters and deck shoes, spry, all of them, for their age.

It was still difficult for Snow to credit the events of the afternoon. He couldn't decide whether what had transpired was sudden, or if for years it had been approaching in increments so slow as to be undetectable as motion to the human eye. How long the world had remained tilted! How slowly his rationality had returned, and how little comfort trailed in its wake. The figure on the beach had intuited his blind confusion before he himself could understand it. "You wait right here," it had instructed him—unnecessarily, since he lacked both the strength and the equilibrium to do otherwise. He'd watched the figure spring into a breaking, thigh-high wave, and when the water receded—taking with it much of the dried clay—he'd stared, uncomprehending, at the miracle. Even after the next, larger wave completed the transformation and the young woman emerged glistening from the sea, he still couldn't make it work.

She had a name—already forgotten—as well as a boyfriend, and once clothed, they'd taken him by the elbow and guided him up the beach. They pointed to each woman they passed who conceivably could've been his wife, careful to ask if he was sure, because he remained confused and disoriented. "I don't think so," he answered after examining one woman with heavy, sagging breasts, another with round, fleshy hips, a third with the wrong color hair. In truth, he was terrified of not recognizing the woman he'd been married to for thirty years, telling them no, and then being wrong. The sun made him feel faint and distant from his own body, and after each new woman proved to be someone else, he'd lost interest in the search, certain that June herself was gone.

In the end it was June who saw them coming, saw her husband looking as if he would surely collapse were it not for the young couple supporting him on either side. She'd risen tentatively, then hurried toward them.

He had seen her without truly recognizing her, occupied as his wandering mind was with the problem of how to explain his delusion, of how to make anyone understand that he'd met Death in the figure of this young woman and been granted what he now felt to be a temporary reprieve. Nor had he thought of a way to apologize to his wife, any more than he had on that terrible day when he and David Loudener had found her, lost and forlorn, staring into that vacant storefront window.

No, June had come swimming into his ken too soon, making him aware of the two young people who were propping him up. And so, with a world of difficult, perhaps impossible things to say, he'd uttered something so cruel that it was easy. "Cover yourself, June," he'd instructed her. "For God's sake."

And so now, Paul Snow, professor emeritus, author of three biographies and a collection of essays, stood at the third-floor window of the Captain Clement waiting for his wife to return, as dusk gathered in the street below. It *was* foolish and arrogant, he had to concede, to think you could imagine the truth of another human life, to penetrate its deepest secrets, as he had been credited with doing in his book on Emily Dickinson. What, in the end, could he know of her heart? Maybe the young man they'd hired to replace him was right to scoff. But there *were* things you could know, even if you didn't want to. Pain, humiliation, fear of inadequacy—these were knowable things. He had known them, felt and shared them, all at once, when he'd told his wife to cover herself. But despite his flaws, he wasn't a different species. Maybe he'd forgotten who June was. Maybe he'd never known. But how exquisitely he who had caused her such pain had felt and shared it in that moment, and was sharing it still.

Down in the empty street he saw a woman who looked like June, though he couldn't be sure, not anymore. She had stopped at a crosswalk, though there was no traffic and no signal, and seemed uncertain whether to head up the street toward him or in the opposite direction. Whoever the woman was, she appeared to be listening, as if to the distant sounds of the sea, perhaps imagining how it felt to be borne gently aloft on a wave.

Poison

I'm not surprised to see that Gene's driving a ten-year-old Volvo, that it's a drab olive green, that it's dirty and bruised-looking. And I'm not surprised that his new wife in the front seat is decently in between homely and pretty. Like the wife Gene recently divorced, this one's the sort of woman of whom it might be said that she'd be pretty if she made an effort. That she makes absolutely no effort is no doubt part of what makes her acceptable to Gene. When she gets out of the car and stands squinting in the sunlight, I see she has the sooty coloration of a mulatto, though I doubt Gene would have failed to mention it if she were black. More likely she's Italian, like he is.

I make a conscious effort not to prejudge her on the basis of what mutual friends have said. "Grim" is the adjective that comes up most often. If Clare were here, I'd say, "She certainly *looks* grim," to which my wife would reply, "No, she looks like someone who's ridden halfway across the country with Gene." I wish Clare were here. I could use a hug.

When Gene gets out of the car, he looks grim himself, which makes me wonder if they've been arguing and their arrival at our door has necessitated a truce neither of them really wants. One of the things I've heard is that Gene's new wife is publicly contemptuous of him, and this woman certainly looks capable of such behavior. But that's unfair. I remind myself that it's late afternoon, which means that they've probably been waiting in the ferry's standby line since morning, which in turn means that they've seen at least three ferries come and go without them. To see that big ferry dock and know you're in the wrong line, well, it isn't easy. It makes you think of all the other boats you've missed, the other things that required reservations you didn't know how to make, or refused to make on principle. And it's no fun sitting there in the hot summer sun trying to gauge what cannot be gauged: how many no-shows there'll be, how many stand-bys will get on, how many times the boat will come and go without you to the place you want to be. Clare and I have warned Gene to be prepared. "It'll be a struggle," I told him. "It may be more of a struggle than it's worth."

"I want to see you," he insisted. "And I want you to meet Portia."

So, they are here, early. I have just enough time to change out of the shorts I'm wearing and into a pair of pants that was hanging on a hook inside the closet door. I start downstairs to meet them, but not before I see Gene bend stiffly and a little painfully at the waist—a sure sign of our shared middle age—and then glance up at the second story of our cottage, as if he's intuited I'm up here somewhere. He's looking at the master bedroom, next to the room I'm in, the one I use as a study. I instinctively step back from the window before he can spot me.

What struck me is what always strikes me when I see Gene again after a long time. He has a head like a mastiff. It's huge, even compared to the rest of his bearlike body. His graying, close-cropped hair emphasizes that prodigious skull. Clare and I differ on the question of what Gene's head is full of. Hypocrisy and bitterness, she thinks, whereas my vote always leans toward injury and rage. We agree on self-loathing, though Clare considers this a sign of his intelligence, while I do not.

We embrace in the doorway, Gene and I, and in that burly hug I am genuinely glad to see him, never mind that I've been dreading this visit. And I can tell that he's truly glad to see me, so I don't pull away—partly because I'm content to be hugged by this old friend, partly because when we're finished I'll have to hug Gene's new wife. In this, it turns out I'm mistaken. Portia pointedly ignores our heartfelt hello and goes over to the sliding door that opens onto the deck and looks out across the stirring grass of the dunes. The ocean beyond is the bluest it's been all summer, almost as if it's been saving this richest, most intense and embarrassing shade for their arrival.

"So," she says, nodding at the view, which is, I admit, breathtaking, "this is how *successful* writers live."

Clare and I bought the cottage two years ago. We'd vacationed on the island for a week or two every summer while the children were growing up, always setting a day aside to look at property we knew we'd have a hard time affording. That we couldn't afford it was something our realtor, Mr. Plumly, had gleaned, and each year he took us around to look at houses with a marginally increased sense of resignation. He seemed to understand that what we described as "our range" was not, in fact, possible for us now, but might be one day, if everything went right. Though he never questioned our right to hope, he clearly saw us as a long shot, at best. Each year he showed us half a dozen new prospects, devoting an entire afternoon to the task, somehow not wanting to just cut us loose—and in doing so set in motion the sort of unlikely harmonic convergence of good fortune that we'd been waiting for.

At the end of those afternoons we'd always sit in the parking lot near his office, looking out across the harbor, the masts of anchored vessels as still as in a postcard. He always asked us how things were going. He knew I was a writer, and apparently had read, or tried to read, one of my books, since he seemed to know what I was doing wrong. "More sex," he advised. "More violence. Violent sex and sexy violence." He claimed to check the best-seller list every time he visited the village bookstore, hoping to see that one of my books had slipped on (by mistake, he seemed to imply).

In truth, we were probably doing better than Mr. Plumly imagined. For all his realtor's intuition, he couldn't have guessed that he was dealing with such fiscally conservative people. Because neither Clare nor I had any experience of money, we never imagined we'd have very much, and when it started coming in, we couldn't believe it would continue to. We were careful with it, suspicious of it, and tried not to get used to it, preparing for the inevitable day when it would be gone. We even discovered that our fathers had the same favorite saying: "Money talks. It says goodbye." We had children and college expenses, and knew that everything cost more than you thought it would, and figured the future held more of the same. So, as we sat in the harbor parking lot each summer contemplating the decent advance I'd be getting for my next book, maybe even the possibility of a small film option, we ended up feeling our own reservations as well as Mr. Plumly's reservations about us, and would decide yet again that this was not the time. On our way back to our rental house we made gentle fun of our realtor and ourselves. "You need more sex," Clare would say, to which I would reply, "More violence."

And then Mr. Plumly's long shot came in. A young fellow who'd never published anything before wrote a novel that mysteriously crept onto the list. More mysteriously still, the studio that bought the film rights decided I was the man to write the screenplay. "You're the only man in America who can do this," the producer told me. "You're the only one who knows what the fuck it's like. You can write this son of a bitch from the inside."

He was referring not just to my half dozen mid-list novels and two unproduced screenplays, but to my blue-collar background in a mill town. The tough-guy profanity was meant to suggest that he was hip to guys like me who could write from the inside. "How about the author?" I suggested for the sake of argument. "It's his book. I bet he could write it from the inside."

"He's twenty-*eight*," the producer groaned. "Twenty-fucking-eight."

"Okay," I conceded. There wasn't much point in arguing that an author mature enough to write a good novel might also be able to draft a good screenplay. And besides, I'd just be talking myself out of the job.

"Besides," he added, "you're perfect. You'd be *absolutely* fucking perfect if you were Italian."

"I *am*," I told him, "on my mother's side." This happened to be the truth.

"No *shit*," he said, stunned by this revelation, this unanticipated good fortune. "Like I say"—he slipped into Hollywood black dialect here—"you the *man*."

As it turned out, I was and I wasn't. My first draft was hailed as brilliant. What it needed—and only this—was a sharpening of focus. Too many characters. Where had all those characters come from? Well, I said, from the novel. In fact, there were even more of them than I'd used. "Let's see if we can't lose the mother," the producer advised. "She's in the fucking way. She can die of cancer before the story begins. In fact, the movie opens with her funeral. Bingo bango, we're there, right in the credits. That works."

"It might," I said, "if we didn't care about her son's motivation."

The more focused second draft was even more brilliant, and all it needed now was a little doctoring, and the producer said he even had a studio guy in mind to handle that purely cosmetic stuff. Smooth. You had to admire it. It didn't occur to me until after I hung up that I'd been shit-canned, that I was no longer the only man in America who could do this job. As it happened, the script doctor wasn't up to the task either, and six months later the project was in turnaround. Everybody involved was out on his ass, including the producer, who apparently wasn't the man either, at least not in the eyes of the studio's new head. A funny place, Hollywood. Here I'd worked on the project for almost a year and didn't have a thing to show for my participation, except for a third of a million dollars. More than I'd made on my six novels combined.

The house Mr. Plumly wanted us to buy with all that money was a three-story contemporary on the southern tip of the island, left unfinished when the real estate market slipped into recession and the builder went belly-up, leaving the house's innards—plumbing, electric, drywall—exposed. "Visualize it," Mr. Plumly advised us, the impressive sweep of his hand taking in all the exposed plumbing and electrical conduits. We were surveying the shell of a house from the uppermost of its three wrap-around decks, the ocean a stone's throw below. Kicking a dead bird under a sheet of plywood, he then guided us through the house's twelve cavernous rooms. "You can lowball him and get the property for two hundred, spend another two finishing the house, and when the market rebounds you sell it for a million and put over half a million in your pocket."

It was momentarily tempting, the way things sometimes can be when viewed through eyes not your own. But we opted instead for a two-bedroom, gray-shingled Cape out-island, secluded at the end of a narrow, rutted dirt lane, among rolling hills and orchards that sloped down toward the ocean. Clare and I agree about most important things, and this, clearly, was what we wanted. It wasn't that I couldn't imagine the huge contemporary finished, I told her, "just that I can't imagine myself living in it."

Clare had given me one of her wry smiles when I said this. "I know what you can't imagine," she said knowingly. "And what you really can't imagine," she said, "is Gene visiting us there."

There is a cool midafternoon breeze out on the deck, and Gene has pulled on a ratty, moth-eaten sweater from the navy-issue duffel bag we'd hauled from the Volvo into my study, where there's a foldout couch. Clare and I are leaving tomorrow for Europe where we will rendezvous with our son, who's pretending to study there. Once we're gone, Gene and Portia can move into our bedroom, though I'm not sure they will. Gene, a writer of subtle, knowing short stories, will be sensitive about climbing into our bed with his new young wife. On Clare's pillow he will sniff something unwelcoming, perhaps even disapproving, and I'm not sure what fragrance he'll find on my own.

"Gene has sweaters without holes in them," Portia says languidly, taking a sip of beer and tilting her head over the back of her deck chair, her long hair hanging free. She shakes it, then straightens up and studies Gene from beneath heavy, hooded eyelids. My own presence on the deck, I suspect, is not strictly necessary to their ongoing drama. Portia already seems perfectly at home, and to her the pillows in our bedroom will smell of bleach and fabric softener, nothing more. "He thinks of this as his Thoreau sweater. The badge of welcome poverty."

Gene is drinking white wine and munching sunflower seeds from a baggie he got from the car. "Thoreau was a fucking tourist," he remarks. "Poverty was a game to him."

Portia turns her languid gaze on me. "Nothing is a game to Gene," she says. "He's *very* serious."

I decide that the best way to befriend my friend is to pretend I like this woman, so I force a smile and nod. "Gene and I go way back," I tell her. What I mean to say is that I know all too well that for Gene nothing is a game, but it comes out sounding like I understand her husband a hell of a lot better than she does.

"Then you know," she says, reaching for his big paw and giving it a squeeze. "It means he's a proletarian writer laboring in the sweatshop of tough, honest prose. It means he comes from an ugly mill town and that's who he is and always will be."

Gene grins good-naturedly, and I suppose even he would have to admit that this is precisely what the sweater connotes. If he doesn't like her tone, he offers no sign. She gives him an unpleasant, birdlike peck on his hairy knuckles and says, in a baby-talk voice, "Isn't that right, sweetie pie?"

What I'm wondering is whether she's aware of having been chosen for pretty much the same reasons as the sweater. At fifty, Gene's still a good-looking man, and women have always been attracted to him. They seem to like his lumbering gait, even like his huge mastiff's head. He's always been pursued by graduate students although he has not, until now, allowed himself to be cornered. Of course until recently he's been married. Even so, it's revealing, if not particularly surprising, that it's *this* woman who has snared him. It's as if he's chosen her to reflect his sense of worth. This will also be Clare's take, I'm sure. And now that I think about it, I realize I'm a little annoyed with her for not having returned.

I go inside to fetch some cheese and crackers, and when I return, Gene looks up at me expectantly. "You should read Portia's work," he says when I set the plate down on the table.

"I'd like to," I say, and it's true, I would, if only to find out whether she's as unpleasant on the page as she is in the flesh. Writers are often surprising in this respect, and it's possible that Portia possesses a more generous self that emerges when she's in the company of people who live in her head.

"She was the only one in the workshop not looking away," he explains, a classic Gene comment if ever there was one. A great believer in "staring down the truth," he admonishes his students not to blink, not ever. Such advice appeals to them, and he has a huge following at the midwestern university where he teaches. He often sees more in his young writers than they see in themselves, and that's either flattery or faith, depending. In this case he's explaining why he's chosen this young woman to be his mate. His twenty-year marriage went south, according to Gene, because Maryanne had never come to terms with who he was and where he was from. The context—his term—remained foreign and strange to her. The spooky part is that I know what he means.

"Her stories were on a different plateau," Gene's saying. "One where pain and loss and betrayal were part of the equation."

Portia, who appears to be pondering the truth of this, turns to me and says, "Does that path go to the beach?"

I say it does, and she scrapes her chair backward along the deck. "Don't," she says when I start to stand up, then she goes inside for an old pink towel she must've got from the duffel bag. "I'll be back."

"Also," Gene says, smiling proudly, "she was the only one in the workshop who was impossible to compliment."

We watch until Portia disappears into the dunes. "It's true," he continues, pouring wine into his glass. "She made me admit she wasn't beautiful before she'd even go out with me."

I fill my own glass with beer, the bubbles springing into existence at the bottom and then racing to the surface. I myself have never made any claims about the necessity of staring down any truths. Indeed, blinking has always seemed to me the most natural, perhaps essential, of human functions.

And so we sit, two friends on the downside of a notoriously slippery slope. Fifty years old. Then the wind shifts, and we can hear the waves rolling in.

Because of the surf, we don't hear Clare until the glass door on the deck slides open and she joins us. She and Gene embrace warmly, and I can't help smiling. After all, my wife and I have had a twenty-five-year disagreement over him that we're not even close to resolving. What I'm smiling at is that, at this moment, I could convince her. The things Gene says are often impossible to take seriously in his absence, and later tonight, when Clare and I are alone, I won't be able to defend him. Right now, though, confined on our small deck with us, his presence and conviction command belief. The same is true of what he writes. Hearing Gene read in public, you are often moved to tears, while on the page these same words lack his power.

Clare seems to acknowledge all of this when she sees me grinning at her, and in return she makes a face. After she finishes hugging Gene, I get one too, a real hug, as if to apologize for leaving me alone for so long. In a glance at the table she's taken in that I've drunk three bottles of beer, a lot for me these days, and that Gene is on his second bottle of wine. She knows right where we are.

Though delighted that she's finally home, I'm unwilling to let her off the hook. "We were about to send out a search party," I say.

"I drove out to the point and bought a lobster," she explains, pouring herself a glass of white wine. "Right off the boat."

"Don't tell me," Gene says. "Lobster sauce?"

"If you're good," Clare tells him.

"Dear Lord, make me worthy," he says.

"Nobody's *worthy* of Clare's lobster sauce," I say. "Like grace, it cannot be earned."

"Unlike grace," Gene says, "it occasionally comes my way."

The lobster sauce, when I think about it, is an inspired choice, given that it so deftly negotiates the shoals of

Gene's personality. Whereas lobster for each of us would have been a conspicuous display, ill suited to the reunion of the sons of mill workers, the lobster *sauce,* served over pasta, signifies a sophistication that is nonetheless mindful of who we are. Until you get to know Gene, it's easy to offend him unintentionally. Which is why I laid in good but affordable Italian wines for his visit. He considers French wines an affectation, and imported beers are always sure to provoke a sarcastic comment. No, Clare's lobster sauce is just the right thing, its ethnic accent overpowering upward mobility.

"Should I get started?" Clare asks, more of me than of our guest, though it's Gene who answers.

"Relax," he suggests. "I'm content to anticipate for hours."

"Portia is investigating the beach," I say, since I know Clare must be wondering.

"We're still in that beginning stage," Gene confesses. "Testing limits. Finding out how much is *too* much. It's harder for her. She needs to carve out her own territory. To keep herself separate from me, her work from my work. She fears it's my intention to revise her."

Clare and I nod seriously. This is the sort of talk that Clare will mimic to devastating effect once we're alone. Gene makes such observations so seriously that in the moment of their expression they seem valid. When they're repeated, in Clare's voice, I will hear something fundamentally insincere. As we pull up the covers tonight, Gene will seem God's own fool, stuffed full of psychobabble. The emotional stage he's describing so plausibly, even generously, will remind us of nothing in our own experience. During the final year of Gene's marriage, which had ended in an ugly, rancorous divorce, he'd called me several times to explain not only his own emotional stages but Maryanne's. In fact, he was most eloquent about *her* pain and rage. "I'm not letting myself off the hook," he assured me. "I'm a damaged man. I've damaged her." When I hung up and tried to do justice to Gene's view of things, Clare's response had been immediate and eloquent. A lip fart.

The three of us talk agreeably for a while, avoiding the land mines that often punctuate these conversations with Gene. A certain amount of mild criticism does come my way, starting with his fear that I intend to give up "real work" for writing screenplays. Worse, he can't understand how I could have quit teaching. Still, these criticisms are couched in flattery. The way Gene sees it, our discipline is full of charlatans and well-intentioned incompetents who not only don't help but can even do real harm to young writers, poisoning fertile ground. I am one of a handful, he claims, who can do apprentice writers some good. He seems almost to suggest that my defection means that he will now have to take on my students, increase his own burden. I tell him the truth: that when I quit last year, I wasn't the teacher he remembered from the residencies we'd shared, that I'd grown tired of repeating myself, sick of the sound of my own voice. That's only part of the truth, of course. I'd quit when I could afford to, something I know better than to say to Gene.

When Clare finishes her wine, she gets up and

announces that she has to get started on the sauce. I follow her inside to get another bottle of wine and a beer from the fridge, but what I'm really after is a moment alone with her. I have sensed an emotional sea change out there on the deck, and when I come up behind my wife and slip my arms around her waist, I can tell from the tenseness in her body that I'm right. I never mind Gene's gentle reproaches, but Clare always does. She's already warned me that she will brook no criticism of our house or the fact that we can afford to own it—certainly not from someone who's getting to use it rent free for two weeks.

"I'm glad to see you," I say, kissing her neck and immediately feeling better.

"I bet you are," Clare says, peeling the thin skin off a clove of garlic.

"You're a good-looking older broad," I tell her. It's one of my favorite lines and sometimes it loosens her up. I recall what Gene said about Portia refusing to have anything to do with him until he admitted she wasn't beautiful. Clare's needs are pretty much the reverse. She enjoys and always has enjoyed being told that I think she's lovely. Her enjoyment seems natural to me, and I wouldn't have it any other way.

"Good-looking or not," she tells me, "this older broad is getting steamed. If he accuses you of selling out to Hollywood I'm going to put an ice pick through his lung and send him out with the tide."

"He won't," I assure her, and, since I could be wrong, add, "and neither will you."

"You let him get away with too much."

"Maybe he's my conscience," I suggest, trying the idea on for size.

When she turns in my arms to face me, I can see she doesn't think it's a great fit. And I'm grateful when she says, "Oh, please."

I carry the beer and wine out onto the deck where Gene has turned in his chair to look out over the dunes toward the strip of deep blue ocean beyond. Since this is also the direction his wife took over an hour ago, I conclude that he's gazing into an uncertain future. And I become aware that the incision on the inside of my thigh has started throbbing.

When I plop back down in my own chair, his trance is broken. "We stopped home on the way here," he says.

By this he means the town we grew up in, and I realize how wrong my conclusion was. I should know by now that his concern runs only in one direction, which is toward the certain past.

Gene pushes his wineglass to the center of the table. "I need a glass of water," he says, pushing his chair back.

"There's bottled in the fridge," I tell him. "The tap water's not so great out here."

"It can't be any worse than what we drank growing up," he says, not unexpectedly.

The mill where our fathers worked, Gene has told me on the phone, has recently reopened after nearly a decade's shutdown. For half a century, chemical by-products were dumped into the river until the water tasted like brass and the fish grew tumors the size of golf balls. As did my father, who grew one of those golf balls in his brain and died a man nobody could recognize, and who himself could recognize nobody, including his son.

It's been my intention to nurse this beer, but I've nearly finished it by the time Gene returns with his glass of tap water, and my head now contains a seed of distant pain which I can tell will grow and bloom.

"How's your father?" I ask, since Gene won't mention him otherwise. The last I heard, he was still living there in the house where Gene was raised.

"We visited the oncology ward," Gene says, throwing me until I realize the "we" here is Gene and Portia, not Gene and his father. "I invited him to come see all the people he poisoned, but he wasn't interested."

Gene's father had been a foreman and later a shift supervisor, a company man to the marrow of his bones, and it's this that Gene can neither forgive nor stop rebelling against. Only tenure protects him from being fired from his university, whose policies, political practices and investments Gene protests loudly, in and out of the newspaper.

"I wanted Portia to see," Gene says, staring at his ice cubes as if the amount of toxin in them might be gauged by the naked eye. "I was honest with her about who I am. She knows she's getting damaged goods." He looks out to sea. "But I wanted her to see the long shadow of the mill."

I stifle an unkind smile. For if Gene were to see it, he'd certainly realize that I consider his new wife yet another facet of that shadow.

Clare slides the glass door open and wonderful aromas waft out onto the deck.

"Should we go find Portia?" I ask her.

"We've still half an hour at least," she says, leaving the decision to me and returning to the kitchen.

"I wouldn't mind taking a little walk," I tell Gene. "Just to see if I can."

There are three or four houses along the path to the beach, all grander than our own, and I'm grateful that they put our modest property into a context that Gene can appreciate. There's our kind of money, and then there's *real* money. He's eyeing these houses with undisguised contempt, as if he already knows and loathes who lives in them. As he most likely would. I've called several neighbors to explain that strangers will be staying in our house for the next two weeks. I made a special point of alerting a quarrelsome man named Connor with whom I've had a couple of run-ins. Our stretch of beach is private by statute, though of course the island's handful of cops can't enforce it when people ignore the signs and stroll the three miles up from the public beach. Connor is rumored to have set his dogs on such trespassers, even to have chased them off in his dune buggy.

When we climb the last dune, I'm pleasantly distracted by the scene before us—the sun a few degrees above the water, miles of deserted sand in either direction, the crashing of the waves. Indeed, it has even broken through Gene's morbid focus, which is itself on the order of a natural force, like sun and tide and wind.

"Wow," he says, taking a deep breath of salt air. "This is just perfect."

"I wish," I tell him. "We had hypodermic needles washing up here last summer."

Gene nods, looking almost relieved to hear it. "That's

what people need to realize," he says, "that no place is safe. That mill gets repeated a thousand times over."

So much for interrupting Gene's focus. I'm scanning the deserted beach for signs of Portia, but there aren't any. With the sun almost resting on the water, I can't be sure, but I think I see a solitary swimmer a hundred yards or so down the beach. I'm about to suggest that we head off in this direction when he says, "We could shut it down, the two of us."

I blink at this. Gene is watching the waves break, and for a brief moment I wonder what he's proposing.

"The city editor would be behind us," he assures me.

It dawns on me that Gene's talking about the mill, and with this realization come two others—that he's crazy and that his lunacy has stirred something in my settled heart, something that could make a lie of my present life. Or if not a lie, one of Gene's famous stages. This moment might, if I so chose, mark the end of my domestic stage. My children are grown and I could leave the rest of this existence—my wife, this house—and complete the circle by returning home with my old friend to wage that final, unwinnable battle with the past.

Gene's looking at me keenly, as if reading my mind. "We could do it," he says, then adds, after a pause, "Maybe we're the only ones who could."

And I do know what he's thinking. The last time I was home, the shabby little downtown bookstore had a huge display of our books, Gene's and mine, in the window. These days, if I was recognized on the street there, it would be due to my vague resemblance to the man on the book jackets, with so many books given as Christmas presents, as reminders that the mill isn't the whole story. That a town this size could produce not one but two authors, however modest in their accomplishments, is a matter of civic pride.

"What makes you think they'll do things the way they used to?" I ask, trying to sound objective. "What about the environmental regulations?"

Gene snorted. "Dumping was never *legal*."

"Still."

"They're getting bold again. Think about it. Republicans running everything. They think they have a mandate. It's okay to poison people again."

We have come a fair distance along the beach. I turn to make sure Portia hasn't materialized behind us, but see there's only our footprints.

Then Gene says the wrong thing, as he always does, eventually. "It'll give you a chance to square things with your old man."

What this is about, I realize, is not *my* father but his own. This public act would be Gene's final repudiation of the company man. Back when we were in grad school together, testing the possibilities and rewards of literature and activism, he asked me late one night after we'd drunk too much bourbon and smoked too much dope, "How can you sit here with me?" When I confessed to not having a clue why I shouldn't, he said, "You're telling me it doesn't bother you that my old man poisoned yours?" My response—"Not a bit, Gene"—had been the wrong one, and not just because he'd misunderstood my flip drunken tone. By denying that he shouldered any inherited guilt,

I'd refused him the possibility of expiation. By giving me a chance to "square things" he now means for me to show the bastards that the world has changed and they don't have the power anymore. We'd make my father's eternal rest easier, and show Gene's that in the end he'd backed a loser.

The problem here is that what I left unresolved with my father is not what Gene imagines. He'd been diagnosed during the early years of Vietnam, and when I drove home from college to see him, I had expressed my view that what was happening to him had been happening for years to the entire nation, which had been force-fed moral poison that was now proving fatal. It was autumn and as we took a slow walk I talked constantly until we ended up down by the stream where we leaned on the iron railing, my father staring down into the swirling eddies of the black water beneath us while I looked off through the bare trees at the dark, satanic mill, thinking more about William Blake than about my dying father. "Well," he finally said, "it's true they poisoned me. But where would a man like me have been without that mill?" He was too kind to ask what logically followed, which was where I myself would be were it not for my father's employment. Of course, I acted out my part, lobbing the obvious rhetorical question back at him. Did any one group of men have the right to poison another? Carried in the subtext of this question had been another, more mean-spirited one. I was asking my father what kind of man allowed himself to be poisoned. Wouldn't such a man deserve his fate?

I pull a deep painful breath into my bought-and-paid-for lungs. "I don't know," I confess to Gene, and boy, is *that* ever the truth.

We have stopped walking, in deference to the gravity of our subject, I assume, until I notice the pink towel and the pile of clothes at our feet. Gene is staring off, one hand shading his eyes against the sun, and I'm blinking and grateful for the opportunity to shade my own eyes. Nearly blind, it takes me a while to see Portia, waving, quite a distance out, and it occurs to me that I didn't warn her about the undertow. I squint into the sun, trying to determine if she's in trouble, then she stops waving and starts swimming toward us. For what seems a long time, I can't be sure if she's making progress or whether there's a possibility that we might be watching Gene's young wife drown. "Is she . . ." I begin, preparing mentally to go in after her.

"Don't be embarrassed," he says proudly. "Modest she's not."

That it takes me so long to make sense of this remark suggests that I've drunk too much, and that the beer isn't mixing well with the antibiotics.

When Portia emerges, dusky but glistening, from the surf, I find myself looking away.

"Isn't he sweet?" Portia says, a little unkindly it seems to me, when she notices.

We turn in early—Gene and Portia pleading road weariness, Clare and I a dawn ferry reservation—and I've fallen asleep watching a book program on public television. I can't have slept more than twenty minutes, but still managed to dream vividly—a predictable symptom, for me, of too much alcohol.

I'm surprised to find Clare warmly in bed beside me, since when I drifted off she was doing last-minute packing. A small phalanx of suitcases is lined up along the wall by the door. "Too bad you fell asleep," my wife says. "You were just alluded to."

"No kidding?" I say, staring at the television as if some atmospheric residue of this might be lingering on the screen. "In what context?"

"In a generally favorable context."

"I wasn't accused of selling out?"

"No, you were accused of a certain realism."

"Ah, well, that . . ." I say.

Dinner had been uncomfortable. Portia, under the influence of Chianti and lobster sauce, was openly critical of Gene, first wondering why he'd published so many books of short stories, then speculating on what it meant that he's never attempted a novel—"loaded up the shotgun," as she put it, and gone hunting bigger game. Now, according to Portia, he was even looking for excuses not to write stories. And that, she concluded, is what the mill obsession is really all about—an excuse. "Gene's always been a good writer," she concluded, "but not a great one, and that's what he's coming to terms with."

In fact, her unpleasantness, coupled with Gene's uncharacteristic reluctance to spar, resulted in the unimaginable—Clare's rising to his defense.

"I thought time decided the question of greatness," she said.

To which Gene smiled and replied, "Oh, no. I'm afraid Portia decides."

After dinner, Gene and I went out onto the deck once more before calling it a night, Portia having already gone upstairs.

"She'll be up all night writing now," Gene said.

"Really?" I was surprised. "She doesn't seem to be in a very good mood."

"Her rage is a source," he said, "that I taught her to tap into." When I said nothing in response, he added, "Hell, it's the source of *our* work too, yours and mine both."

There it was again, the old camaraderie Gene had first extended nearly three decades ago, the year I arrived to begin my graduate work and he finished his own degree. He was glad I was there, he kept insisting, so there'd be two people who knew what life was really like. It's what he's always wanted of me, all these years, an acknowledgment of how similar he and I are.

Which reminded me of a conversation I'd had with the producer of the script that had paid for the island house. When he approached me, he said I was the only writer he wanted for the project, implying that if I didn't do it, he might just let the whole thing slip into turnaround. Within a few short months, though, he'd forgotten this lie. When complimenting me on my first draft, he hadn't neglected to congratulate himself. "I *knew* you were the guy," he said. "If you hadn't done it, I'd have had to go to that Ruggieri asshole. You know him?" When I said I did, he sighed significantly. "He's an okay writer, but he's got no fucking sense of humor."

I fell asleep in my clothes, so I get up to undress. Clare watches, and when I climb into bed she remarks that the incision doesn't look as puffy or angry today. Clearly, the antibiotics are working. Why the incision should have become infected to begin with is a great mystery to everyone, my doctors included, but it's a mystery I've been instructed not to worry about. I'm a lucky man, they insist. The tumor was benign.

"I gather you didn't say anything to Gene," Clare observes.

"I didn't see any point," I tell her, and I know she understands that what I mean by this is, Why give him any fuel?

We are quiet then, and Clare snuggles close. I'm almost asleep again when she says, "Do you want to go back and shut down that mill?"

This surprises me. Usually she knows what I want without asking. I'm the one who has to ask.

"I have no idea," I tell her. "I'll think about it, I guess."

"Maybe he'll let it drop," Clare suggests, zapping the TV with the remote. I'd turned it on fearing raised voices in the next room, though it's quiet in there now.

"Gene?" I say. "He's never let anything drop yet." We are silent in the darkness for a while. "I had a strange dream," I confess.

Clare kisses my shoulder, stroking my belly with her fingernails. "You always dream when you drink too much."

I smile. No one knows me better than this woman. In fact, it wouldn't surprise me if she knew *what* I'd dreamt while being alluded to on television, that I was walking along our stretch of beach and stepped on a needle, and then the sand was suddenly bristling with them and I was punctured again and again as I limped home, feeling something new and toxic coursing through my veins.

The Mysteries of
Linwood Hart

OBJECTS

When Lin Hart announced his intention to play American Legion baseball, his mother had to swallow her mis-
givings. For years she'd been referring to him as her little
philosopher because he was prone to reveries from which
he emerged with some of the strangest questions she'd
ever heard, the most recent of which was, Did objects
have desires? Like what? she said. A lamp? You're thinking maybe a lamp *wants* to shine? "Possesses an active
interior life" was how the boy had been assessed at
school. Her own assessment was that Lin was the kind of
kid you had to remind to look both ways before crossing
the street, not once but every time he left the house; so
now that he was riding his bike all over town his mother
was hearing automobile horns in her sleep. And why this
sudden interest in baseball, anyway, a sport that featured
a lot of standing around between pitches, pauses in the

action that would encourage his too frequent lapses into abstraction, then injure him with its eruptions of violent action? She just hoped he wouldn't be picking his nose when the baseball hit him.

Like so many things, this was his father's fault. Thomas had got him a baseball glove for Christmas, determined to provide an athletic alternative to the scholarly genes his son had inherited from *her* family so powerfully that the rough physicality of the Harts had been driven deep into latency. Which was as it should be, as far as Lin's mother was concerned. If the boy's Foster blood was settling some genetic argument in favor of something more refined and civilized, this was hardly cause for regret.

At age ten, Lin himself had not given much thought to these characteristics of his family tree, though he would have conceded he was prone to philosophical rumination. His leisurely reveries, if he thought about them at all, seemed perfectly natural. "Hasn't it occurred to you," his mother remarked, her brow knitted in concern after he'd given voice to one of his odd queries, "that somebody would've thought of it already if it were true? Millions of people have lived before you. What makes you think *you'd* be the first to think of something? That's what I'd like to know. What do you think you are? Special?"

Lin understood that this was a rhetorical question whose answer was supposed to be "No," even though, most of the time, he thought it might be "Yes." It was hard to imagine that all of his personal thoughts had already *been* thought. When he lay on his stomach in the grass and watched an ant climb up one side of a blade and then down the other, his truest sense of things was that in the world's long history, no one had ever witnessed this *exact* event, and he couldn't help feeling special to have done so. Why shouldn't his thoughts be special, too? What if he was right to think them, even if no one else had?

For instance, why *shouldn't* inanimate objects be capable of desire? Take leaves. They wanted to dance, didn't they? He understood that it was caused by wind, of course, but this didn't explain why they didn't all get up and dance with each new gust, instead of just certain ones. Leaf A would rise and do its jig while Leaf B, right next to it, wouldn't even stir. The ones dancing in this gust might rest during the next, and to Lin, this meant they were expressing a desire. And Wiffle balls. Their frantic wiggle after leaping off a plastic bat suggested a similar desire, though his father, who at the moment wasn't living with Lin and his mother, explained that the symmetrical holes cut into the plastic sphere were responsible for the ball's erratic and exciting flight. Okay, but to Lin's way of thinking, the holes merely set free the inner spirit of the ball.

Baseballs might not want things as badly as Wiffle balls did, Lin allowed, though they were certainly capable of expressing desire. When a ball struck his stiff new mitt, he could feel it searching desperately for an exit. When it hit in the webbing, the ball immediately tried to burrow out the heel, and when it hit in the heel, it seemed to know that it had to climb out through the webbing. Covering one exit with his bare hand merely ensured that the ball would spin and lurch toward freedom in the other. Even if they weren't as exuberant as Wiffle balls, it was clear that baseballs, left to themselves, preferred not to be caught.

At times, the secret desires of inanimate objects were clearer than people's yearnings, adults' in particular. Before his father moved out, Lin would wake up in the night and hear him asking his mother, "What do you *want* from me, Evelyn? Could you tell me that? Just what the *hell* do you want?" Lin listened hard, but he was pretty sure his mother never answered this question. Sometimes he'd come upon her unawares and she'd be staring off at nothing and shaking her head and muttering to herself, "I don't know. I just don't know." Lately, she'd taken to listening to a popular record by Jo Stafford, who sang about how the wayward wind was a restless wind that yearned to wander. If you didn't put the skeletal arm of the Victrola directly over the spindle, the record would just keep playing, over and over, which seemed to suit her fine. According to what she said, his father couldn't answer that question either. Sure, he could be charming, she admitted, and fun to be around, but when it came to knowing what he wanted out of life, he didn't have Clue One. Were all grown-ups like this?

MR. CHRISTIE

Of all the adults Lin knew, though, his American Legion coach was the most perplexing. During the week Mr. Christie painted houses for a living and always wore paint-splattered overalls and a Boston Red Sox baseball cap. On Sundays, hatless and bald except for the pale fringe around his ears, he looked so different that for a long time Lin hadn't realized that the two men were one and the same. Dressed in his starched white shirt, clip-on tie and a sport jacket, his smooth cheeks scented with aftershave, what did Mr. Christie *want* when he reached the long-handled collection basket all the way down the pew to where Lin and his mother sat? If it was just their weekly offering, why did the basket linger there, as if he secretly was hoping for something else?

When the eight rosters had been announced and Lin had learned that he'd be playing for Elm Photo, Mr. Christie's team, he'd immediately wondered if the coach had asked for him. He hoped so. Maybe their church relationship meant that Mr. Christie would grant his wish to play center field. The form that came in the mail and required his mother's signature had inquired what position each boy hoped to play. Lin's father, who now had an apartment over the barbershop downtown and saw him only on weekends, had said the best player usually played center field, so he'd signed up for that. He wasn't sure he'd be the best player, but thought he probably would be, because he loved the sport and saw himself in his mind's eye ranging gracefully under a blue sky, high fly balls settling into his new glove. In preparation for American Legion, he'd been playing backyard Wiffle ball all spring long with the neighborhood kids. Afterward, every night in his bedroom, he tossed a baseball-sized rubber ball over his shoulder and then lunged after it, imagining his soft tosses as hard-hit line drives. With each dive he landed full-length on his bed, where he bounced hard but always managed to hang on to the ball. He'd have played this game much longer, making one game-saving catch after another, except all that thudding got on his mother's nerves and after a while she'd call "Enough!" up the stairs and warn him what would happen if he broke his box spring.

That he might *not* be the best player on Mr. Christie's team occurred to him only when he arrived for practice that first day and saw that he was one of the smallest boys there. Playing catch, they seemed to be hurling the baseball at each other as hard as they could, and it made an angry, popping sound in their mitts. They were all public school boys Lin didn't know. He attended the small Catholic grade school in town. His father had not approved of this, but his mother taught in the public schools and knew what went on there; she had insisted that their son enroll in St. Mary's. As new boys arrived, they propped their bikes up against the chain-link fence, slipped their soft fielder's mitts off their handlebars and joined the double line, leaving Lin to marvel at how easy it was for them. He kept hoping some other kid from St. Mary's would turn up, but none did. So he leaned up against the fence and just watched, waiting for an invitation, though not one of the other boys so much as glanced in his direction.

When Mr. Christie arrived in his pickup truck, the first thing he did was gather his team into a semicircle and read from the forms they'd filled out several weeks before. It quickly became apparent that every boy wanted to be pitcher or shortstop or outfielder. "Lin Hart, center field," Mr. Christie read from Lin's form. Was it his imagination or did some of the other kids grin at one another knowingly when he raised his hand? Actually, center field hadn't been one of the choices listed on the form. He'd drawn a line through "outfield" and penciled in "center field" for the sake of clarity. If Mr. Christie found this amusing, he didn't let on. In fact, he gave Lin the same friendly smile he offered all the other boys, never letting on that he knew Lin from church.

"How come you've got a girl's name?" one of the boys asked.

"That's L-Y-N-N," Mr. Christie explained. "Lin here is L-I-N. Short for Linwood, would be my guess."

Lin, red-faced, nodded his head, grateful to Mr. Christie for intuiting his full name and for not making a big deal out of the other boy's insult. "Well, Lin, we can try you out in the outfield if that's what you want, but you look to me like a natural second baseman."

Lin shrugged, torn between his original idea and the fact that his coach had recognized some special quality in him. Besides, something about Mr. Christie's tone of voice suggested that a second baseman wasn't such a bad thing to be, not if that's what you were naturally. From where they were all sitting along the first baseline, center field looked a long way off, much farther from home plate than it was playing Wiffle ball in somebody's backyard, and Lin wasn't sure he could throw a baseball that far. He told Mr. Christie he supposed second base would be fine.

"That a new glove you got there, Linwood?" the coach asked, beaming at him.

"Don't worry, you'll grow into it," his father had said when Lin tried the glove on. They'd gone out for spaghetti at Rigazzi's on Christmas Eve and this was where he'd opened his present. Try as he might, Lin couldn't get the mitt to close.

"It's a good one," his father told him, as if that explained why. "So take care of it, and don't leave it out in the rain."

"I won't," Lin promised.

"Okay then," his father said, apparently relieved to get these issues cleared up. After dinner, they drove back to the house where they'd all lived together until that fall, when his father moved into the apartment above the barbershop. When Lin started to get out, his father said to hold on a minute, and they waited there at the curb for several minutes. What they were waiting for, Lin supposed, flexing his new glove with both hands, was for his mother to notice the car and invite his father to join them for the rest of Christmas Eve. Being Catholic, they were separated, not divorced. His mother's position was that his father could come back and live with them again as soon as he grew up, but not until. His father had predicted that his mother would kiss his ass before he'd ever walk through that door again. Both of these, Lin had concluded, were highly unlikely events.

"Well," his father said, staring at the house, "Merry Christmas then."

MATHEMATICAL PROBABILITY

For the first week, Mr. Christie divided the team into three groups and held separate practices: the pitchers and catchers one day, the outfielders the next, then finally the infielders. Two or three boys idled around each base, awaiting their turn to field a grounder. With so many boys, it would've taken quite a while between turns, even if Mr. Christie hadn't kept dropping the bat and pulling on his mitt to demonstrate the proper position to field a ground ball. Lin paid attention for as long as he could, but then allowed his thoughts to wander. What had been puzzling him for some time was mathematical probability as it applied to his coach. The problem was this: Mr. Christie was one of four ushers at the eleven o'clock Mass that Lin and his mother attended on Sunday. Each week she gave her son the envelope—Lin happened to know there were two dollar bills sealed inside—for him to deposit in the long-handled wicker basket, but how did it always happen to be Mr. Christie leaning into their pew? Always arriving just before the services began, Lin and his mother had to take seats wherever there was room. Although the church had four aisles, no matter where they ended up it was always Mr. Christie who accepted their offering, and he always gave Lin a wink as if to acknowledge a special bond between them.

Before Lin could come to any conclusions about what this bond might be, he heard Mr. Christie call out, "Look alive out there, Linwood!" This hurt his feelings because it sounded like a criticism even before anything had actually been required of him. But once the ball leapt off Mr. Christie's bat, he realized that it wasn't a criticism but a warning. The baseball seemed to generate sound not only by thumping along the hard infield dirt but also by cutting through the air. There was time for just two quick thoughts. The first came in the form of a question: If Mr.

Christie was so fond of him, why had he hit the ball so hard? The second arrived as a decision. True, it was clearly his name that had been called, but it seemed to Lin that he should feign confusion and pretend that he thought this ball rightfully belonged to the boy standing next to him. In the split second it took him to step aside, he very nearly convinced himself that this heartfelt wish was fact; there was also just enough time for the ball to find an infield divot, change direction and express, it seemed to Lin, its innermost desire, which was to belong to Linwood Hart and not the boy standing next to him. When it hit him squarely in the forehead, Lin sat down hard, right on top of second base, the ball suddenly inert on the ground between his legs.

Being hit didn't hurt as much as it surprised and frightened him. What scared him most was the sound the impact had made inside his head, as if a snare drum had been struck between his ears, and the sound continued to reverberate as he sat there on second base, his eyes watering, his nose suddenly running like a faucet. Even worse than the *sound* was the odd sensation of things *moving* inside his head at the moment of impact. He'd always imagined that the human head, or at least his own head, was solidly constructed and all of a piece, whereas it now appeared that things were actually floating in it, that he himself was one of the things that floated there. Until being struck by the baseball, he'd always considered his head a safe place to hide out. Now he wasn't so sure.

"*That's* the way to get in front of it," Mr. Christie called out encouragingly. "Stand up and dust yourself off, Linwood. Here comes another one."

ENEMIES

Namely Hugo Wentz. A sixth grader, one year ahead of Lin at St. Mary's, Hugo joined the team almost two weeks into the season. The rules were specific: no one whose application form was not handed in by the deadline would be allowed to play American Legion, but an exception was made for Hugo because his father owned Elm Photo. In fact, it was rumored Mr. Wentz had enrolled his boy himself, so he wouldn't be such a sissy. Lin recalled a day that winter when the fifth- and sixth-grade boys had been combined for gym class to have their fitness evaluated. Many of the boys had been able to climb hand over hand up a thick rope all the way to the rafters, and Lin had made it over halfway. Hugo was the only boy who hadn't been able to pull himself up the rope at all.

The other members of the team were already playing catch, waiting for Mr. Christie to show up with the bats and bases, when Lin heard a vehicle bumping along the rutted access road. He turned, expecting it to be Mr. Christie's pickup, but instead it was a brand-new 1963 Cadillac with tail fins, coming toward them too fast and stirring up a cloud of dirt when it stopped. Hugo sat in the front seat, as far as possible from the man behind the wheel, who put the car in Park and stared across the seat at his son.

From where he stood against the fence, Lin had a good view of the Wentzes, who greatly resembled each other. Mr. Wentz was a florid man, all belly and jowls, who owned several small, unrelated businesses in town. Perhaps because he was always flitting back and forth between them, Mr. Wentz managed always to convey a cosmic impatience. What he seemed impatient about right that instant was that his son was just sitting in the car, looking straight ahead, almost as if he hadn't noticed they'd stopped, or as if the arrival at their destination had to be announced, like on a train. Finally, after his father's lips moved, Hugo got out of the car, closed the door behind him and gazed impassively at the chain-link fence. Though there was no gate, the fence was no more than waist high. Still Hugo regarded it as if it were twenty feet tall and strung at the top with barbed wire. After a moment, the window of the Cadillac rolled down and Mr. Wentz called, "Forget something, Hugo?"

Apparently his son was still grappling with the problem of the fence, and the expression on his face suggested he couldn't handle both it and his father's question at the same time. Either that or he'd concluded that the two things were somehow related. Was his father asking him if he'd forgotten how to fly? Only when Hugo finally turned around did he see his father was holding his mitt. Mr. Wentz, disgusted that the boy had made no move to fetch the glove, Frisbeed it at the boy, who juggled it, then dropped it. The mitt remained there on the ground while father and son stared at each other. At last, Mr. Wentz said, "What?"

"There's a fence," Hugo said.

His father rubbed his temples with his thumbs. "So climb it," he said, and then roared off. Hugo watched the Cadillac until it shot between the stone pillars that marked the entrance to Carling Field, then tossed his glove over the fence. Lin assumed he was going to take his father's advice and climb it, but he was wrong. Instead, Hugo shambled its entire length, down to the hinged gate a hundred yards away, where he let himself in and then shambled back. To Lin, these two gestures made no sense. If he wasn't going to climb the fence, why toss the glove over it? Having watched both his going and his coming, Lin suddenly felt grateful that Hugo Wentz was on the team, if only for the purpose of comparison.

When the pathetic circuit was finally completed, Lin pretended to be deeply involved in evaluating the team's talent, perhaps even deciding on a starting lineup, so he wouldn't have to play catch with Hugo Wentz, who probably threw like a girl. Still, after a minute or two, he sensed the boy's presence behind him.

"Hey, Hart. You got a ball?" Hugo wanted to know.

Lin shook his head, surprised that the other boy knew his name and had chosen to use it.

Hugo Wentz snorted unpleasantly. "Figures," he said, turning away again.

It nearly took Lin's breath away, that one word. Just that quickly, it seemed, he'd made an enemy.

GRANDMA HART

Shortly after moving into the apartment above the barbershop, Lin's father had gotten into a car accident. By the time he got around to telling Lin's mother about it, she'd already heard. "Totaled, huh?" Lin heard her say

into the telephone. "Well, now you're a foot, like me."
That not having a car made a person into "a foot" made a
kind of sense to Lin, who saw no reason to suspect he
hadn't heard his mother correctly. The expression certainly made more sense than another of her favorites,
which was along the same lines. Often, befuddled, she'd
proclaim she didn't know whether she was a foot or horseback anymore.

His father claimed that not having a car was no big
deal. His apartment was only a few blocks from the hotel
where he tended bar in a waist-length jacket and bow tie,
his shiny black hair combed straight back, looking wet
even when it was dry. It did mean that they had to borrow
Uncle Bert's car when they visited Grandma Hart, who
lived alone now, since Lin's grandfather died, one town
away. Because his father and Uncle Bert weren't speaking, it also meant that it was Aunt Melly who came out
onto the porch to hand over the keys. "You could come in
and have a cup of coffee, Thomas," she said, cradling her
belly. Lin tried to remember if he'd ever seen his aunt
when she wasn't pregnant.

"Not likely," his father replied. "Wasn't for somebody
who'll remain nameless, I wouldn't be here at all."

Lin understood that he himself was the nameless person, and also that the reason his father and his uncle
weren't speaking had something to do with the car—but
also that it was not *just* the car, according to his mother,
who had little use for any of the Harts, claiming that to
them, fighting was as natural as breathing.

A couple of months before, Uncle Bert had phoned

Lin's mother to complain. "Listen to me carefully, Bert," he overheard her say. "You've got nothing I want, and that includes your car." When apparently Uncle Bert tried to backtrack, she continued, "If you don't want your brother to borrow your car, tell *him,* not *me.*"

Lin could hear his uncle's whiny voice leaking out of the receiver.

"I don't *care* what he says, Bert. If he's using it to take Lin places, that's between you and him. If he owes you money, same deal. You've known him a lot longer than I have, and if you're dumb enough to give him anything you want back, you've only yourself to blame."

"Lin might like to come in and see his cousins," Aunt Melly said now, though nothing could have been further from the truth. Lin's cousins, all three of them, were nasty creatures with streaming noses and sagging diapers who wanted him either to pick them up or let them sit on his lap, which always left a smelly wet spot on his pants.

"Besides, you could say hello to your brother and patch up this silliness."

"I'm right here, if he wants to patch anything up," his father said. "And he knows where I live. If I can walk all the way over here, he can drive over there."

"Have it your way, then," Aunt Melly sighed. "I'm too worn out to try to convince either of you. I used to be pretty before I met your stupid family." And suddenly it seemed to Lin that she might cry.

"You still are," his father said. "Why do you think you're knocked up all the time? Because you're ugly?"

This brought a small smile. "Yeah, but what about later, when he decides I'm too fat."

"Come find me, darlin'," his father suggested. "Looks like I'll be free."

"I might, just to see the look on your face when you open the door and see me standing there with four brats in tow," Aunt Melly said, though Lin could see that she'd cheered up when she tossed his father the keys.

"I'll have it back by supper," he said.

At Lin's grandmother's, things began where they always did. "Why don't you ever come visit your grandmother?" was what she wanted to know. Lin understood that the old woman was really asking his father, not him, but it was still weird and embarrassing to stand there in her kitchen and hear this same question first thing.

"Give it a rest, Ma," his father said, sinking onto a kitchen chair. "We just walked in the door and already you're at it."

Lin didn't like his grandmother's house, where it was always too warm and full of food smells he didn't recognize—because according to his mother, she was "ignorant" and insisted on cooking with onions and never opened the kitchen windows to air the house out.

"Your grandmother's not going to live forever, you know," she said, still fixing him with her stare. "When she's dead, you're going to wish you came to visit her."

No I'm not, Lin thought.

"Tell her she's full of it," his father suggested, stretching his long legs out in front of him, crossing his feet at the ankles. Since Lin had not been offered a seat, he was still standing there in the middle of the bright kitchen.

"Tell her if they dropped an atom bomb right in the center of town, she'd be the only survivor."

The old woman looked her son over. "What's that?" she finally said, pointing to a purple swelling under his right eye. Lin was glad she'd asked, because he'd been wondering about it himself.

"Nothing."

"Nothing," she repeated. Then, "Why don't you go work for your brother Brian?"

"Why don't you mind your own business?"

"He called yesterday. Said you could come to work for him whenever you want."

"Good. It's settled, then," his father replied cheerfully. "When I want to, I will. Right now, I don't want to. Right now what I'd like is a cup of coffee, if that's not too much to ask."

"I hope you don't talk to *your* mother like this," the old woman said to Lin. "Is this any way for a man to talk to his own mother?"

"Go ahead and take her side," his father suggested. "If you don't, she'll be mean to you too."

"You want a soda?" she said. That was the only good thing about Grandma Hart's house. The refrigerator was always full of orange sodas, a brand he'd never seen anywhere else. At his other grandmother's he got one glass of name-brand cola, after which it was fruit juice. Here he could drink all the off-brand orange soda he wanted.

Later, back home, sitting at the curb in Uncle Bert's car, his father was pensive, as he usually was when they returned from their weekend afternoons together. "They're not bad people, you know," his father said, though when he said it he was staring at the house where he used to live, so Lin didn't understand who he was talking about. And he couldn't help wondering if Uncle Bert had called his mother again, since instead of returning the car when he'd promised, his father had driven to a tavern where he knew everybody and their dinner kept getting interrupted by people who wanted to know where Lin's mother was and how much longer they were going to stay separated. "You'd have to ask Evelyn," his father said. "Call her up right now, in fact. If you find out anything, let me know."

"Who?" Lin said now, responding to his father's remark about bad people.

"Your grandmother. Your Aunt Melly."

Lin shrugged. It wasn't like he'd ever thought they *were* bad people.

"Your Uncle Bert's a pain in the ass, but he's not a bad guy either."

Lin nodded. Actually, he liked his uncle the best of all his father's relatives, though his mother was right: his whiny voice was just like a girl's.

"It wouldn't kill you to pretend you liked them, is all I'm saying."

Lin considered this. His impression was that he *had* been pretending this very thing.

"Just because your mother doesn't like somebody doesn't mean you can't," his father continued. "Just because she thinks she's better than everybody doesn't mean you have to."

"Okay," Lin said, suddenly on the verge of tears.

"So, is she seeing anybody?"

"Who?"

"Who."

"Mom? No."

"She ever say anything about me?"

"She says she doesn't want to be married to a bartender."

He nodded. "Well, that's a switch. Her favorite people all used to be bartenders. That was before you, of course."

Back inside the house, his mother called to him from the kitchen. "Is he gone?"

"No," Lin said, peering through the blinds.

"What's he doing?"

"Just sitting there."

"He'll get tired of it," she said.

GHOSTS

Lin understood, sort of, about the past—for instance, that his mother was different before he was born. True, it was odd to think of her as somebody whose favorite people were bartenders, but to Lin, this was further evidence that his dramatic entrance into the world had changed everything. It felt, sometimes, as if the world must've been patiently waiting for him to get born so that *real* things could start happening—kind of like the difference between the drills at school and an actual fire. He knew that things could and did happen even if he wasn't there, but he still had the impression that the truly important events tended to occur only when he was there to witness them. Last year, for example, when his parents argued late into the night about maybe moving to Connecticut where there were good schools and his mother could make better money teaching, Lin always woke up and listened to their voices coming up through the heat register. It was possible, he supposed, that he'd slept through other arguments, but he imagined that by their very nature (as witnessed by the fact that he'd not been there to take them in) they would not be essential to his understanding or survival. Surely life played that fair, at least. The world was there for him to learn from and learn about. Otherwise, what was the point?

True, his faith that the world was considerate of him was occasionally undermined, like when his father finally moved into the apartment above the barbershop. Lin had felt that he'd probably missed some important event or discussion that would've provided a bridge to the moment when his father appeared at breakfast with his suitcase to explain that he'd be going away for a while. And when he tossed the suitcase into the trunk and drove off in the car, Lin felt even more powerfully the existence of some ghost scene from which he'd been mysteriously and unfairly excluded. He knew that in his mother's opinion the stupid Harts were holding his father back, whereas according to his father, his mother was a "daddy's girl"—complaints he'd heard voiced through the heat register. But what had happened to bring things to this current pass? He couldn't conjure the missing scene, no matter how hard he tried, which begged a question: What if the world *didn't* play fair? What if it didn't care whether he learned its lessons or not?

One Saturday morning in July, Lin's mother decided it was time for his haircut, and they'd walked downtown, she dropping Lin off at the barbershop so she could run some errands. As he waited for his turn in the chair, Lin tried to imagine his father's apartment on the second floor, a place he never had visited. He'd asked about it once, but his father had told him not to worry, he wouldn't be there that long. As a result, the apartment was somehow less real than it would've been had he been allowed to see it; though Lin had no idea why this should be so, nevertheless it felt true. On television he'd seen movie sets—whole streets that were mere facades, doors that led into empty space—and he suspected something of this sort about his father's apartment.

The barbershop was quiet except for the snicking of Tony's scissors and the occasional turning of a magazine page, so Lin was able to hone in on the ceiling and listen for the sound of his father's footfalls, some sign that reality and not illusion was up there above the shop. After his haircut, with lime-scented cologne stinging the back of his neck, Lin waited outside for his mother and studied the second floor's unshaded windows and the dark doorway around the corner that led upstairs. Just inside, at the foot of the stair, was a broken beer bottle, which proved that his father didn't live up there, not really. The fact that his mother never even glanced at the entryway when she returned from her errands suggested the same thing.

They walked home in silence, Lin trying to think how to ask his mother if she, too, sometimes doubted the actual existence of places and things she'd heard about but never seen. Perhaps it was because he was so deeply involved in this metaphysical query that he felt the world tilt when they turned into their street. There, high up on a wooden ladder and dressed in his painting clothes, Mr. Christie was scraping the eaves of their house, and again Lin registered a ghost scene in which worlds merged dangerously.

"Good morning, Evelyn," Mr. Christie called down when he heard them climbing the porch steps below. "How you doing, Linwood?"

And there it was—the same expectant hesitation that occurred on Sunday mornings when Mr. Christie leaned down the pew with the offering basket, implying some other hoped-for thing.

"You've got a lot done already," his mother observed, holding a hand up to shield her eyes from the sun.

"The worse the peeling, the easier the scraping," Mr. Christie said, as if to suggest that the worse something looked, the easier it was to correct. "The back'll go slower."

"Where's your partner?"

"Paul? Oh, he came down with some bug or other. Don't worry, though. You won't be charged for two men unless two men are here." Then to Lin, "That's some haircut you got there, Linwood."

Lin could feel himself blush at being observed so closely.

"He hates going to the barber lately," his mother said, and this made him redden even further. Next would she explain why? That he hated sitting in the chair and thinking that maybe his own father was right overhead?

"Be glad you have to go," Mr. Christie said, confusingly until Lin remembered that under his Red Sox cap, he was bald. "You should come to one of Lin's games, Evelyn," he then said, and Lin could feel his mother bristle. She didn't like people making suggestions about what she should or shouldn't do, especially after his father moved out, an event that caused a lot of people to voice their opinions. "Lin's our star second baseman."

"I would, but Carling Field's so far," his mother said, "and I don't have transportation."

"Oh," Mr. Christie said, as if anticipating this excuse. "I could swing by and pick you up. I think there'd be room for all three of us in the truck."

"Well, it's certainly nice of you to offer," she said, starting inside, as Lin wondered why, if it was such a nice offer, she wouldn't even entertain it.

Upstairs, after lunch, Lin watched Mr. Christie from behind the sheer curtains of the front window and tried to imagine the missing ghost scene. Had his mother hired Mr. Christie over the phone or had he called her to ask for the job? And why hadn't she mentioned that the house needed painting? Outside the window, Mr. Christie's paint-splattered boots were so close that if the screen hadn't been there, Lin could've reached out to untie them. Strange, he thought, to be so close to another person when that person had no idea you were even there. From where he crouched, he could hear every swipe of the scraper as the paint flecks rained down, many of them coming to rest on the sill. Each time Mr. Christie reached out from the ladder, he made little grunting sounds, and once he said, "There. Gotcha, you little devil." At that moment Lin realized he himself was, for Mr. Christie, a ghost presence, both there and not there. Would it be possible, Lin wondered, for someone to get so close to him without him noticing? In the barbershop, for instance, would it have been possible for his father to watch him through a small hole in the ceiling? No, he decided, it didn't work that way. Where the world was concerned—he felt this deeply—Linwood Hart was privileged.

COST

"That Howard Christie up there?" his father wanted to know the next day. Their Sunday afternoon was already off to an unusual start, his father having arrived in Uncle Bert's car instead of the two of them walking over there to pick it up.

Mr. Christie had finished scraping the front and was painting now. When Lin acknowledged that this was precisely who was on the ladder, his father nodded thoughtfully. "Figures," he said. "He always was a bird dog."

"What's a bird dog?" Lin asked, but his father had already gotten out of the car. He now stood on the brown terrace, hands on his hips, sighting up the ladder, standing there until Mr. Christie noticed him.

"Hello, Thomas," he called down, friendly, like he always was. "You and Linwood off to the lake?"

That morning after Mass, Lin had mentioned that he hoped this was where his father might take him that afternoon.

"Didn't know housepainters worked weekends, Howard," his father said.

Mr. Christie chuckled. "Well, it's kind of a short season, Thomas. You get a stretch of good weather, you need to take advantage."

"Well, if that's your story, you should stick to it," Lin's father said. "You wouldn't be charging my wife any time and a half or anything, would you?"

"No, nothing like that, Thomas." Mr. Christie was still smiling for some reason. "In fact, she's getting my discount parish rate."

Now it was Lin's father's turn to chuckle. "I might want to see the bill, just to make sure."

Mr. Christie turned back to painting now. "I keep an open book. Anybody that wants to can have a look."

"Well, I might want to."

"You and Linwood enjoy your afternoon."

His father looked like he might have liked to continue this conversation, but apparently he couldn't think of a way, so he got back into Uncle Bert's car. The key dangled from the ignition, but he made no move to turn it. "Your mother inside?"

Lin said she was. His father nodded, staring darkly at the front door. His prediction—that Lin's mother would kiss his ass before he ever entered that house again—was weighing on him heavily, Lin could tell. He could probably predict—as could Lin himself—what his mother would say if he'd walked in right then: "Did somebody kiss your ass, Thomas? Because I have to tell you, it wasn't me." When his father finally decided it wasn't worth it, he looked over at Lin, really taking him in for the first time. "What happened to you? Join the marines?"

"Haircut," Lin explained.

"No kidding," his father said. "He call you Linwood all the time?"

Lin admitted he did.

"If you don't like it, tell him."

Lin said he didn't mind. His name, he knew, had always been a bone of contention between his parents. He'd been named after Grandpa Foster, whose own father had also been named Linwood. "I'm just grateful he wasn't named Jitbag," Lin had once overheard his father remark. Lin was glad, too. Though he had no idea what a "jitbag" might be, he didn't care for the sound of it.

They immediately headed in the wrong direction for the lake, and Lin had just concluded they were in for another long afternoon at his grandmother's when they passed the street they would have turned on if her house had been their destination. In fact they kept on going right out of town, finally pulling into a used-car lot out by the new highway. In its center was a tiny shack that looked like an outhouse, and a man wearing a plaid sport coat—who'd been leaning back on the hind legs of a chair and reading a magazine by the light of the open door—got to his feet and came out to greet them. "Slick Tommy," he said wearily, as if the very sight had exhausted him. Quite a few of his father's acquaintances referred to him as "Slick," which made Lin wonder if maybe this was the reason he didn't want to move to Connecticut, where nobody would know his nickname.

"How about this one?" his father wondered, indicating a bright green Bonneville.

"Just took it in trade."

"And?"

The man shrugged. "I wouldn't, if it was me."

"I'm not you."

"Ain't that the truth."

"What do you need to get?"

"Twenty-four hundred."

His father made a face. "I meant the other price. The one you give your preferred customers."

"You know who my preferred customers are, Tommy?" the man said. "They're the ones who buy cars from me. Not the ones who come in every week and tell me I'm a thief and never buy so much as a hubcap."

His father looked around the empty lot. "You want me to wait here while you tend to all your other customers?"

They took the Bonneville for a ride out on the high-way, his father pushing the accelerator all the way to the floor and letting up only when the speedometer hit 85, the engine rumbling and throaty, clearly disappointed when it started slowing. Then they drove over to Uncle Bert and Aunt Melly's, parking the Bonneville out front. To Lin's surprise, when his father tooted Uncle Bert himself came out onto the porch (causing Lin to suspect yet another ghost scene), followed by Aunt Melly and all three of their kids, the smallest one toddling right over to Lin and throwing up her arms.

"She likes you," Aunt Melly translated. "She wants you to pick her up."

Lin regarded the child's full diaper, her runny nose and crusty chin. When he finally picked her up, the child stared deep into his eyes, gumming and twirling her pacifier provocatively.

"I don't know, Tommy," Uncle Bert said in his whine when his father started the Bonneville up, its engine rumbling and straining like an animal on a leash, drawing the neighbors out onto their sagging porches.

"It's got pretty good pep," his father said.

Uncle Bert shook his head as if he'd once had a car just like this one and had to shoot it. "Probably gets about eight miles to the gallon. Pop the hood a minute."

The next-oldest cousin now wrapped his arms tightly around Lin's thigh and buried his shaved skull in Lin's groin, which, for reasons entirely mysterious to Lin, gave him an erection.

"That's some haircut you got," his aunt said. From previous visits Lin knew that she wasn't about to rescue him from the affection of his cousins.

"Smells hot," Uncle Bert said when Lin's father finally located the latch and lifted the hood. "What are they asking?"

"Twenty-four," Lin's father said.

"I don't know," Uncle Bert said again, still staring at the engine as if expecting it to reach a decision.

"It's not nice to touch people there, Bertie," Aunt Melly said languidly when she noticed that her son, curious about the hard shape in Lin's pants, was trying to determine its exact size with his thumb and forefinger. Now the oldest girl came over too. Only a couple of years younger than Lin, she stared at him with the same vacant expression her father was using on the Bonneville's engine.

"*Jesus*, Melly," Uncle Bert whined, finally noticing Lin's predicament. "Can't you take them inside?"

"They get tired of being inside," Aunt Melly said. "Besides, all that TV isn't good for them."

"Why don't you let Brian sell you a car?" Uncle Bert wondered. "He'd make you a good deal."

"Because then I'd owe him."

"So what? He's your brother. He made me a heck of a deal on the Buick."

"Right," his father said. "As he points out every time you run into him."

The vacant-eyed girl now jumped on Lin's back, wrapped her spindly legs around his waist and covered his eyes from behind with two damp hands.

"The trouble with you Harts is you're all stubborn as mules," Aunt Melly observed as she headed back inside. "Bert, sweetie, what'd Mommy just tell you?"

"If you'd go to work for him, he'd probably give you a company car," Uncle Bert pointed out.

"He'll kiss my ass before I'll ever work a day for him," Lin heard his father predict. With the child's hands clamped tight over his eyes, he couldn't see a thing.

"Well, I don't know if I'd buy this," Uncle Bert said. "Not at that price."

"Oh, they'll come down some."

"Still."

Lin could sense that his father had turned toward him now. "Okay," he called over, "put those kids down. It's time to go."

The salesman in the plaid coat was bouncing from one foot to the other when they pulled back into the lot. "I was just about to call the cops," he announced when they got out.

"The car I left here was worth a lot more than this gas-guzzler." Lin's father pointed at Uncle Bert's Buick, sitting right where they left it.

"That's true," the salesman conceded. "Except it's not yours. It's your brother's."

The two men stood looking at the Bonneville. Lin's shirtsleeve still had a smelly wet spot where he'd balanced the toddler.

"So, what do you think?"

"Runs hot, too," Lin's father said.

The man nodded. "That Chrysler you drove last week was twice the car."

"Should be, at twice the price."

"Well, the better something is, the more it costs. You've probably noticed that yourself, Slick."

"So what do you really need?"

"On which?"

"This one."

"The one that guzzles gas and runs hot?"

"Right."

"I suppose I could let it go for two grand."

"How about if I was somebody else? Like one of your golfing buddies?"

"If *you* were somebody *else*?" the man sighed. "What a wonderful world this would be."

AFFECTION

Mr. Christie wanted to make a catcher out of Hugo Wentz, until the boy's father went ballistic at the suggestion. Mr. Wentz drove the Caddy right up behind the backstop, got out and read Mr. Christie the riot act over the fence, as Hugo sat in the front seat with the grim expression of someone who, if allowed to redesign the world to his own specifications, would retain very little of the present one. Only when his father, having told Mr. Christie how it was going to be, got back in the car did Hugo get out, toss his glove over the fence and begin his long solitary trek to the distant gate and then back again, as his father fishtailed through the stone pillars.

Lin watched the whole thing from second base, wondering first why Mr. Christie allowed the other man to speak to him that way, and then why he didn't seem to hold it against Hugo when he finally arrived back at the diamond and promptly sat on his glove where he'd tossed it in the grass.

"Come on out here, son," Mr. Christie called, then added, when the boy stood up and started walking, "and bring your glove with you. We're going to try you at a new position."

That Mr. Christie treated Hugo Wentz so kindly was puzzling to Lin, who couldn't think of a single reason why he should. Bestowing affection on a boy that fat, sullen and sarcastic called into question the value of affection in general and devalued the affection afforded boys who'd earned it. Lin understood that Mr. Christie was quick to smile, to encourage and forgive, but there had to be a limit, didn't there?

Which was why, when Mr. Christie welcomed Hugo to the pitcher's mound—of all places—and put a hand on the boy's shoulder while pointing out home plate to him, Lin found himself disliking not just Hugo but also Mr. Christie, and he made a mental note right then to refuse his offer of a ride home. Since he'd started painting their house on weekends, Mr. Christie had taken to giving him a lift after practice, laying Lin's bike carefully in the bed of his pickup on top of the canvas duffel bag that contained the bats and balls. A couple of times they'd even stopped at the DQ for soft ice cream. Mr. Christie had a way of asking questions so that Lin didn't mind answering, and of nodding at all his answers as if they were the very ones he himself would have offered. Never did Lin feel more at the center of things than in Mr. Christie's presence, which was why, last week at the DQ, a terrible wish had occurred to him before he could prevent it, a wish he'd regretted immediately and which frightened him so badly that, needing to be alone, he'd gone to bed early that night, even though his mother kept coming in to check on him, convinced he was coming down with something. What scared him was that a careless wish, especially from *him*, might possess some untold power.

At least that wish was something he didn't have to worry about now, not after seeing Mr. Christie's hand on

Hugo Wentz's shoulder. Having finished his instructions to the inattentive boy, Mr. Christie now trotted in from the mound and donned a catcher's mask, telling another boy to grab a bat.

Lin found it even easier to dislike his coach and sometime friend in the stupid catcher's mask, the man who just last week he'd wished was his own father.

"Look alive out there, Linwood," he called out jovially, though Lin was aware of having done nothing to merit this warning. When Hugo Wentz's first pitch sailed halfway up the backstop, provoking laughter throughout the infield, Lin joined in, not really caring if Mr. Christie might be disappointed in him.

PERSONALITY

One Saturday in early August, Lin and his mother took the bus to New York and then a train out into the Connecticut countryside, where her parents lived in a house with a swimming pool. Before they left, she'd gotten into an argument with his father because the trip meant he'd miss his afternoon with Lin. They were taking the trip, his mother explained, so they wouldn't have to listen to Mr. Christie banging his ladder against the house all weekend, peering into whatever windows he was painting around. It was like living in a fishbowl, she said, though Lin had never seen Mr. Christie look anywhere but at the brush massaging paint into the dry wood. The job was taking too long, she also claimed, because Mr. Christie was doing it by himself. He said his regular partner was still sick, but she'd seen the man on the street and he looked perfectly fine.

Unlike Lin's other grandmother, Grandma Foster didn't pester him constantly about why he didn't come to visit her more often. She seemed to understand that there were things a ten-year-old boy couldn't be held responsible for. Unlike Grandma Hart's house, Grandma Foster's was big and airy, and with the windows thrown open, breezes ruffled the curtains even on the warmest days. That two women the same age could be so different was baffling to Lin, who liked to think that age and experience would naturally lead to similarity. How did human beings turn out so different? The older people got, it seemed to Lin, the less they agreed on. According to his mother, the reason was personality, which, to his way of thinking, didn't so much explain the problem as just give a name to something that still didn't make any sense.

He spent most of Saturday afternoon in the pool doing cannonballs off the diving board while the adults talked inside. He quit only when the sun slanted behind the roof of the house and the breeze turned cool. When he complained of hunger, his mother reminded him that Grandma and Grandpa Foster ate late, like civilized people. They liked to have cocktails first. His grandfather must have overheard part of this conversation, though, because a few minutes later he appeared on the deck with a big platter of steaks, and the new gas grill puffed to life; to ease the wait, Lin was given a stick of pepperoni to gnaw on, but only after he'd washed his hands and face.

That night, as always, he slept in the downstairs den, on a sofa that folded out into a bed. The room had its own television, which he was permitted to watch as long as he wanted, but his hours in the pool had wearied him and before long he was asleep. He woke up once—someone had come in to turn the TV off—at the sound of voices from the foot of the stairs. "It's not about the money," he heard his grandfather say. And then, "What you saw in him in the first place is what I'll never understand."

When they returned home late the next afternoon, his father was waiting for them at the bus stop in Uncle Bert's car. Lin's mother had been preoccupied during the entire journey, and when she saw the Buick, she looked like this was the last straw. "What're you *doing* here, Tom?" she said when he picked up her bag.

"What," he said, dropping the suitcase on the curb as if he'd suddenly lost his grip on the handle, "you'd rather take a cab? If you do, just say so, because there's one right across the street."

"I thought we'd agreed you weren't going to meet us."

"Really?" he said, tossing the bag into the open trunk and then slamming it shut. "You thought we agreed about something?"

Lin sat in the backseat, his mother up front with his father. "How's Linwood the Third?" his father said. "Still convinced he's better than everybody?"

"Don't start," his mother warned him.

"Daddy's little girl," his father chuckled.

To Lin's surprise, his mother didn't say a word. In fact, she didn't speak again until they pulled up to the curb behind Mr. Christie's pickup. "Good Lord," she said under her breath. "He's still here."

"Well," his father replied, "that's love for you."

This remark made no sense at all to Lin, who wasn't sure he'd heard it right.

"You want me to get rid of him?" his father offered.

"No. I just want him to be finished."

"Well, I'm going to take my son out for a plate of spaghetti, if you have no objections," he said. "You're welcome to come too, if you like."

"What I'd like," she replied, getting out of the car, "is to go upstairs, climb into bed, fall asleep and wake up far away." Lin knew exactly what she intended to do when they were gone. She would put Jo Stafford on the record player and let "The Wayward Wind" play over and over.

"Things don't have to be like this, Evelyn," his father called, watching until the door grunted shut behind her. Then he swiveled around to look at Lin. "You want to come up front?"

Lin shrugged. Nobody, he'd noticed, ever asked him about anything that had any consequence.

"Fine," his father said. "Stay there, then."

Actually, Lin realized, that wasn't quite true. Mr. Christie not only asked his opinion but also listened carefully to it. Why then, when at that precise moment the man came around the corner of the house, balancing the big wooden ladder expertly on his shoulder, his hand half raised in a good-natured wave, did Lin pretend not to see him?

SPAGHETTI

They were no sooner seated in Rigazzi's than Lin's favorite waitress, the one who enjoyed giving his father a hard time, came over. "I was beginning to think you'd died, Slick," she said, one hand on an ample hip. "You never come in anymore."

His father pretended to read the menu. "Well, Jolene, I keep running into people I don't like," his father said, indicating the far end of the restaurant where Lin's Uncle Brian sat eating spaghetti with his family.

"Speaking of which," Jolene said, "he wants to know if you'd like to join them."

"Yeah?" his father said. "Tell him I know how much he'd like to spoil my dinner, but I'm not going to let him."

"I'll say no such thing," she assured him.

"Suit yourself," his father said amiably. "I'll have the—"

"Rigatoni and sausage," Jolene finished for him.

"Rigatoni and sausage," his father confirmed as she wrote it down.

Now she raised an eyebrow in Lin's direction. When he opened his mouth to speak, she said, "Spaghetti and meatballs," wrote that down and then snatched the two menus. "I could make other predictions, too, but I'd just depress myself."

Lin wouldn't have minded joining his Uncle Brian's family. His cousin Audrey, who was fifteen, had breasts and was about the prettiest girl Lin had ever seen—so pretty, in fact, that he couldn't even hold it against her that she'd never spoken a kind word to him. His cousin Mackey, who was two years older, did play Wiffle ball with him, but only on the condition that he got to bat first, which meant in effect that Lin never got to bat at all, since he could never get Mackey out. Uncle Brian's problem, according to Lin's father, was that he was a blowhard, and in his own opinion, Mackey was well on his way to becoming another.

"You didn't know that, did you," his father said when Jolene was gone.

"Know what?"

"That Howard Christie's in love with your mother."

Lin thought about the way the collection basket paused each Sunday after he'd put in the offering envelope.

"You thought he just enjoyed painting houses on the weekend?"

Exactly. That was exactly what Lin had thought. Either that or he enjoyed Lin's own company.

"Ask him, if you don't believe me."

Lin tried to imagine circumstances in which he might ask any such thing, and failed utterly.

"What'd you eat at your grandfather's?" his father asked after Jolene had brought their salads.

"Steak," Lin said around a mouthful of iceberg lettuce.

"Figures," he said, nodding thoughtfully. "Your grandmother still drinking?"

"Drinking what?" Though he knew. He'd seen her going back into the kitchen to visit the silver shaker, seen her careful, deliberate gait after dinner, smelled the strange sweetness on her breath when she kissed him good night, the same sweetness he sometimes smelled after his mother listened to Jo Stafford too long.

"Too bad," his father said. "Of course you'd drink, too, if you were married to Linwood the Third. He still trying to convince your mother to divorce me?"

His father had stopped eating and was watching him. Lin would have liked not to answer, but he knew that wasn't an option. "He isn't going to give her money any-more," he said, immediately smarting at this betrayal of his mother, especially since his father seemed cheered to hear it.

"I figured that's how she was staying afloat. How'd she take that news?"

But across the restaurant, his aunt had gotten to her feet and headed to the ladies' room, and Uncle Brian, having finished his meal, also rose and came across the room. He was about the same height as Lin's father, but otherwise seemed much larger and his face was always purple, as if the top button of his shirt was too tight.

"Hey there, big guy," he said, offering his huge hand to Lin.

"Stand up when you shake hands," his father sug-gested, also rising to his feet. "Your uncle's big on manners."

Uncle Brian chuckled pleasantly, as if at a fine joke. Lin was surprised when the two men shook hands, both of them acting like they couldn't have been more pleased to run into each other.

"You didn't want to eat with us?" Uncle Brian said, sounding genuinely hurt.

"You were about done, and we were just starting," Lin's father explained.

"Would've been my treat."

"Well, big brother"—Lin's father's smile got thin—"I may not have as much money as you, but I think I can manage a couple of spaghetti dinners."

"You ever see anybody as stubborn as your old man?" Uncle Brian wanted to know. But before Lin could respond, he'd already turned back to his brother. "That Bert's Buick you pulled up in?"

"What of it?"

Uncle Brian held up both hands in surrender. "Nothing. I just heard you were looking for a car, that's all. Why don't you let me help you out?"

"I'll think about it."

Uncle Brian sighed. "Why does it always have to be this way with you, Tommy, will you tell me that? What the hell did I ever do to you? What did *anybody* ever do to you?"

Jolene arrived with their food then, setting the plates down hard. "If this is going where I think it's going, then take it outside."

"You want to go outside, Tommy?" Uncle Brian was saying now. "Is that it?"

His father just grinned back at him. "I only want two things, Brian. I want to sit down and eat my rigatoni, and I want you to go fuck yourself."

"*Outside,*" Jolene warned, her voice rising now.

"Don't let your spaghetti get cold," Lin's father said. "I'll be right back."

Spaghetti was one of Lin's favorite foods because

it was both delicious and thought-provoking. They'd been coming to Rigazzi's for as long as he could remember, and his father had taught him how to twirl spaghetti on his fork instead of cutting it up. The trick, he'd learned, was to start with just a few strands; otherwise you ended up with a big ball of pasta twine that either wouldn't fit in your mouth or gagged you when you tried to chew. Even though he now regarded himself as an expert twirler, he still liked it that you couldn't predict, when you pulled on one strand, which strand on the opposite side of the plate would snake toward your fork through the giant tangle. Even when you'd eaten most of it, you still couldn't tell what was connected to what. This complexity and surprise was nearly as delicious as the actual taste.

Lin had eaten only a few forkfuls when his cousins suddenly crowded into the booth with him. Mackey arrived first, slipping onto the bench Lin's father had vacated and flipping up the window's wooden slats so he could peer outside, leaving his sister to lean across Lin. Her long dark hair brushed his nose, her body so close he could smell whatever it was she was wearing—perfume, maybe, or just girl's soap.

"They're fighting," Audrey whispered, and sure enough, when Lin looked out through the open slats, his father and Uncle Brian were grappling with each other in the parking lot. His father momentarily managed to get him in a headlock, but then Brian backed him into a parked car, hard, breaking his grip.

"Dad'll kick his ass," Mackey said confidently, letting the slats fall back into place and heading for the front door. When the door opened, Lin heard a far-off siren, and saw Jolene hang up the phone behind the cash register.

Her brother gone, Audrey slid into the opposite bench and regarded Lin critically. "Fighting is *stupid*," she said, again peering out through the slats, opening them just wide enough to see through herself. After a minute she let them fall shut again. "The police are here." When she sighed, her breasts heaved. "What are you looking at?" she said, having caught him.

Lin thought it better not to say.

"How old are you?" she wanted to know, her eyes narrowing.

"Ten."

"You're just a kid," she said contemptuously. "You shouldn't be interested in things like that."

He supposed this was true, but said, "Things like what?"

"Like what girls have under their sweaters." This was an electrifying conversation, but then she went and spoiled it. "You don't see us going around staring at your zipper, do you?"

Lin could feel the blood rush to his cheeks. Blessedly, his aunt came out of the ladies' room just then, looking surprised to find their table empty, her daughter sitting with Lin, her husband, son and brother-in-law nowhere in sight.

"Shall I tell my mother where you were looking?" Audrey said.

Lin was about to beg her not to when he was visited by a sudden, mysterious intuition. She wouldn't tell. She was relishing his discomfort, much as Mackey enjoyed never letting him bat. "Go ahead," he said, surprising himself. To the best of his recollection, he'd never in his life done anything so bold, and it was thrilling to see immediately that his intuition had been correct. When his aunt arrived at the booth, Audrey said languidly, "Dad and Uncle Tommy are fighting in the parking lot."

"How absurd," his aunt said, ignoring Lin entirely. "Your father knows he's got a bad back. He won't even be able to straighten up tomorrow."

In a few minutes Lin's father slid back into the booth opposite him. He had a split lower lip, and there were a few drops of blood on his shirtfront. "You all done?" his father said, seemingly amazed that his fight had lasted long enough for his son to eat his entire dinner. He stabbed a rigatoni and chewed it thoughtfully, wincing when the tomato sauce stung his cut lip. "You don't have to tell your mother about this, you know."

Lin nodded. His father dabbed his swollen lip with a napkin, wincing again, then pushed his plate away and studied him carefully.

"Your cousin Audrey's sure growing up, isn't she?" he finally observed, giving Lin a chill.

HATE

Hugo Wentz's father might have bullied Mr. Christie into making a pitcher of Hugo, but that's where it ended. Though he attended each game and heckled relentlessly from the stands—"Give the other kids a chance, Coach.

You afraid you'll lose your job?"—Mr. Christie continued to do things his own way. He did not like to put his younger boys in pressure-packed situations where they'd feel terrible if they failed, so he was adamant about not putting Hugo into any game without a cushion, preferably a large one. Being ahead or behind by a dozen runs or more, Lin had noticed, made it a Hugo situation.

Since their confrontation on the first day of practice, the two boys had spoken to each other only once. And the conversation, initiated by Hugo, had been one-sided. "My dad knows your dad from the hotel," he said, grinning unpleasantly. "My dad *tips* your dad." Since then, when neither was in the game, they sat on opposite ends of the bench. At first their mutual aversion had been wholly satisfying to Lin, who didn't want to be associated with a boy so pitifully lacking in baseball skills—who *looked* so little like a baseball player. But as the season wore on he began to suspect that Hugo was equally content with the arrangement. Ever since that first practice when Lin had been struck in the forehead by the grounder, he'd remained timid about any ball hit in his direction, and batters continued to beat easy groundouts because he was afraid to charge the ball. As a result he thought he detected a triumphant curl of Hugo Wentz's lip. By midsummer he'd even given up his nightly game of snagging line drives in his room since his heroic fantasy was no longer sustainable. Every time he dove recklessly and smothered a hard-hit liner, landing fully extended on his bed, he'd see Hugo's lip curl and know the truth—that a rubber ball wasn't a baseball, his soft mattress not a hard-packed infield. It was ironic, of course, that his enemy should be the reason both that he no longer loved baseball and that he didn't quit. For as long as Hugo remained on the team, he, not Lin, would be regarded as its worst player. The pure joy was gone, though, and when the final game of the season rolled around, Lin was relieved.

American Legion games, usually high-scoring affairs, were seven innings, and it wasn't until the bottom of the sixth, with a two-run lead, that Lin was inserted as a pinch hitter. The Stop & Shop coach was making similar end-of-season moves, and the boy brought in to pitch to Lin walked him on a full count. By the time the inning was over and Elm Photo took the field, their lead had swollen to four runs. Spirits were running high until Mr. Christie was seen handing the baseball to Hugo Wentz, who started to mope out onto the field without his mitt and had to be called back in for it.

"Bear down now," his father called out from the bleachers as he warmed up. "Those sissies can't hit."

But of course they didn't have to. Hugo Wentz never had any trouble throwing the ball over the plate during warm-ups, but something happened as soon as a boy stood there with a bat in his hands. You could actually see it happening. The first pitch or two might be close to the strike zone, but after that Hugo's eyes would glaze over as if he was watching the game on some inner screen that only he could see and which bore little relation to the one being played on the field. His pitches got wilder and wilder, one in the dirt, the next halfway up the backstop. Unless Lin was mistaken, there was for Hugo just one physical reality once he was on the mound: the sound of his father's voice in the bleachers, a voice that did not take long to grow impatient. Only by plunging deep into something akin to a coma was the boy able to sever that last link with reality.

After loading the bases without throwing a single strike, the coach of the Stop & Shop team called his next batter back to the on-deck circle for a conference, and though he was whispering, it was painfully clear to everyone on both sides of the diamond that his instructions were: Don't swing.

"He's got no stick, Hugo," Mr. Wentz shouted. "Just throw the damn ball over the plate. He couldn't hit it off a tee."

Good advice, Lin thought, but Hugo was no longer, strictly speaking, there to hear it, and his next four pitches were even wilder, the last eluding the backstop completely. The runner on third trotted home, the bases still loaded, nobody out. Next batter, same result.

"Go settle him down, Coach," Mr. Wentz yelled. "Don't you know anything?"

In fact, Mr. Christie was already on his way to the mound, but when Hugo started to hand him the ball, he refused to take it. Instead he turned the boy around so they faced the outfield, their backs to the stands. "Look here, Hugo," Mr. Christie said quietly. "I'll take you out if you want, but I think you can get this man out."

"I hate him," Lin heard Hugo Wentz say. "I *hate* him!" And with that he threw the ball down onto the mound so hard that it ricocheted all the way to first base in the air.

Mr. Christie called for the ball, and the first baseman tossed it back. Then the coach handed it back to Hugo. "I want you to throw it just like that," he said, "except at the catcher's mitt."

Hugo accepted the ball reluctantly. "We'll just lose," he said.

"That wouldn't be so bad," Mr. Christie said. "We've lost other games. But if you throw it just like that, like you're real, real mad, we'll win. Can you throw it like you're mad?"

"Christ on a crutch, Hugo, play ball!" his father yelled. "What the hell's wrong with you?"

"Okay," Hugo said, taking Lin by surprise. "I can do that."

Hugo's next pitch shocked both teams and everyone in the bleachers by bisecting the plate and popping into the catcher's mitt. The umpire was so dumbfounded that he called it a ball, before correcting himself, and Lin could almost see his brain telling him to actually watch the pitches now, which up to this point hadn't been necessary. The next pitch was in the exact same spot, and the batter, now with two strikes, stepped out of the box and stared at his coach, who almost imperceptibly shook his head. When the umpire called strike three in an amazed tone of voice, the batter threw his bat in disgust, and to make matters worse, the runner on third, thoroughly disoriented, came trotting home as if the batter had been walked and then was easily tagged out. This rendered the Stop & Shop coach apoplectic, perhaps because he'd just stood there watching and never shouted for the kid to get back to the bag. Just that quickly there were two outs, and Elm Photo's infield was suddenly full of chatter. "Way to throw strikes, Hugo! One more now! Just like that!"

When he realized that he was the only one on the team not offering encouragement, even Lin joined in, though he was deeply ambivalent about Hugo's sudden, inexplicable discovery of the strike zone. Of course he hoped Elm Photo would win this last game, but would have been just as content if Hugo came in and lost it singlehandedly. At least in this scenario, Lin himself couldn't lose the game for his team, which was his greatest fear. Whereas now, if a ball was hit in his direction and he failed to catch it, the winning run might score on *his* error. No one would remember the five batters Hugo had walked, only that Lin Hart had let an easy out skitter between his legs. Worse, it would end the season, giving him no chance of redeeming himself. That the team should rally so excitedly around Hugo Wentz seemed monstrously unfair.

Yet when he heard Hugo Wentz say "I hate him!" Lin felt a sudden kinship he wanted desperately to deny. Though he didn't hate his father—or anybody, really—the other boy's enmity registered powerfully, like something rancid on the back of his tongue. Because there were things, Lin realized, that *he* hated, hated so deeply, in fact, that he'd never found the courage to utter them even to himself. Despite never having seen it, he hated his father's apartment over the barbershop. He hated the fact that adults couldn't agree on how to do simple things, like keeping the windows open on hot days. He hated his mother playing Jo Stafford over and over, and that dreamy, faraway look in her eye that suggested she'd like nothing better than to follow the wayward wind and leave her whole life, including him, behind. Lately, now that he thought about it, he hated almost everything, even things he'd loved the most, one of which was baseball.

Tasting all this on the back of his tongue, he also realized that he was jealous—could such a thing be possible?—of the pathetic Hugo Wentz, not just because he'd struck a batter out, but because he'd somehow found the courage to acknowledge and express his hatred, and as a direct result had a completely different look about him. Not confidence, exactly. No, he just looked like a boy who'd finally had enough, who preferred to face the firing squad now rather than later. That the batter who now stepped up to the plate was the best hitter on the Stop & Shop team, that he'd already hit two home runs, didn't even seem to occur to him.

It occurred to Lin, though, because the boy was left-handed, and when he took a slow practice swing, the end of his bat was pointing right at Lin, as if to predict where hell would break loose. As Hugo started his windup, things went into slow motion and Lin Hart found he had the leisure to think a great many thoughts. For instance, that the game didn't really matter so much, because everything was changing. A year from now his father might be living someplace else. Hadn't he said from the start that the apartment over the barbershop wasn't forever? No, he'd insisted it was just until Lin's mother made up her mind. New York City, he'd hinted more than once, would be a much better place for a bartender. Or maybe his mother would announce tomorrow that they were moving to Connecticut to be closer to Grandma and Grandpa Foster. Maybe that's why the house was being painted, so it could be sold for a better price. Maybe in another month he'd be in a new school in Connecticut where they had lots of pretty girls even prettier than his cousin, whose hair he could still feel brushing his cheek and whose smell he'd breathed deep within his lungs. He remembered the satisfaction of guessing right about Audrey's bullying, the pleasure of seeing his bold challenge work according to plan. *That's* what he was going to be good at, it now dawned on him. He'd be good with girls. His father was. That's why people called him Slick, and slick was a good thing to be.

Lin had other thoughts, too, and his reverie might have produced a great many other understandings had his thoughts not been interrupted by the sharp crack of a bat.

CENTER

A strange car was parked right in front of the house when Lin returned home that evening, a Dodge that looked brand new. Leaning his bike up against the porch railing, he went over and peered inside, looking for clues, but the interior was clean, with nothing on the seats or the floor except a paper mat on the driver's side.

In the house he found his father, wearing a sport coat and sitting in the chair he'd used back when this was his house too. His mother, all dressed up, lounged on the near end of the sofa, and both held short highball glasses half full of murky liquid. His father's busted lip was swollen, but otherwise he looked perfectly natural, and they were both smiling at him so smugly that Lin was forced to consider the possibility that one of the improbable scenarios required to bring this domestic scene to fruition had actually occurred: either his father had grown up, or his mother had kissed his ass.

His father spoke first. "Who won?"

"How come you're here?" Lin said.

"I live here."

Lin looked at his mother, who nodded, with a crooked smile that for an instant made her look like his Connecticut grandmother.

"Whose car is that outside?" he said.

"Ours," his father smiled.

"How about that?" his mother said. "We're no longer a foot."

And just that quickly, a flash of understanding. "Afoot" was one word, not two. "On foot," it meant.

"Anything else you want to know?" his father said.

There was. The baseball game had run long, making him late for dinner, but there were no food smells. "What about dinner?"

"We're going out to eat," his mother said.

"To Rigazzi's?"

"If you like. Why don't you go get cleaned up and put on some nice clothes?"

"I don't get it," he finally admitted, which struck both of them as about the funniest thing they'd ever heard.

Ten minutes later, they'd climbed into the new Dodge and were just about to pull away when Mr. Christie's pickup rumbled up behind them. Lin's father looked pleased by this turn of events and, ignoring his wife's whispered plea to drive off, immediately turned off the ignition and got out. Lin got out too, leaving his mother the only one in the car. The two men shook hands, Mr. Christie beaming his usual good cheer, Lin's father wearing a knowing grin.

"I guess you're about done here," he said.

"Just stopped by to pick up my ladder and brushes," Mr. Christie said.

"Good," his father said. "Then you'll be gone when we get back."

This remark appeared to sadden Mr. Christie more than anger him. Turning to Lin, he said, "Linwood tell you he saved the game?"

"Lin, you mean?" his father said. "My son?"

Whatever he was driving at, Mr. Christie didn't seem all that interested. "You should've been there," he smiled, and Lin found himself smiling back. Given how things had worked out, they were friends again.

"I will be, from now on."

"Well, that's good," Mr. Christie said, sounding like he meant it. "Today was just the beginning, right, Linwood? Wait'll *next* year. All he needs is to grow a little, and then he'll be a natural shortstop."

Lying in bed that night, Lin replayed what had happened that afternoon over and over, trying to decide if he really had saved the game. It was thrilling to think so, and to know this was the conclusion that everybody else had come to, even if he himself wasn't so sure. The truth, insofar as he was able to reconstruct it, was that he'd been daydreaming when the big Stop & Shop kid uncoiled at Hugo Wentz's pitch, and what followed wasn't at all like his nightly fantasies of snagging line drives. For one thing, he didn't have to dive, because the ball had headed straight for him—was on him, in fact, before he even had time to consider ducking. Rather, his glove had somehow been there in front of his face, and the ball had rocketed into the stiff webbing, closing the mitt around it without Lin even having to squeeze, and then yanking it clean off his wrist. Glove and ball together had described a graceful arc in the air above his head before landing in the dirt behind second base.

Recalling the moment, Lin realized he'd been in no great hurry to retrieve the glove. The batter, he'd concluded, was out, by virtue of the fact that the ball was still right there in his glove. That the glove was no longer on his hand didn't seem all that significant, so he was confused by all the yells coming from both teams, as if everybody had forgotten that this was the third out or else couldn't quite believe that Lin Hart, who always flinched away from slow dribblers, had managed to catch a baseball hit this hard. To prove they were wrong, he picked up the glove, turned toward the umpire to show him that the ball was still in the glove, and, in so doing, collided with the runner who'd been on first and was now bearing down on second. The collision knocked both boys down, but Lin was holding on to the glove with both hands and didn't drop it, which meant that the runner had been tagged out. Naturally, the other boy protested, complaining that Lin hadn't even meant to tag him, but the umpire was having none of it. "You don't have to *mean* anything," he explained. "This is baseball. You just have to do it." Lin repeated this last part in the dark, satisfied, more or less, to have done it.

His parents' voices were coming up through the heat register now, in the early stages of an argument, unless Lin was mistaken. His mother was saying that of course they were obligated to pay Mr. Christie, whereas his father was of the opinion that it would serve him right if he got stiffed. As they moved through the rooms below, the conversation went from inaudible to audible to inaudible again.

Earlier in the summer, Lin would've concluded that he was hearing all the important parts, that nothing essential to his understanding or well-being would be said if his ear wasn't receiving and processing the information. Now it seemed just as likely that the really important things— like his parents' decision to live together again, like his father quitting bartending and selling cars for Uncle Brian, like his mother's refusal to do as his grandfather, Linwood the Third, had asked—would play out quite naturally in scenes that did not require his presence. Coming home from the restaurant, they'd parked in front of the barbershop and climbed the dark, evil-smelling stairs up to the dingy flat to gather the last of his father's things. It was an awful place, but Lin understood it was as perfectly real as every place else in the world, which was large beyond imagining, containing every single place he himself had ever been or never would see in his entire life. Earlier, when he'd been sent upstairs to clean up and change clothes, he'd passed by his mother's room and seen through the open door the unmade bed—his parents' bed again, not just his mother's—and intuited in the

New from

Richard Russo

That Old Cape Magic

It's the end of what seems like a perfectly lovely
wedding weekend on the Cape, but for Griffin, the
middle-aged father of the bride, it marks the
beginning of his descent into a failed marriage, a
confrontation with his parents' deaths, and the
realization that the life he has does not measure up
to the life he thought he wanted. With moments of
great comedy alternating with others of rueful
understanding, *That Old Cape Magic* is unlike
anything Richard Russo has ever written.

Available August 2009 in hardcover from Knopf
$25.95 • 272 pages • 978-0-375-41496-1

Please visit www.aaknopf.com

tangle of sheets at least part of what made the world go round. And he knew that when Sunday came and the three of them were at church, for the first time since last autumn, it would be a different usher who leaned the wicker offering basket down their pew, and that it wouldn't linger there before them like some hard-to-ask question.

It was into this entirely different world that Linwood Hart now fell asleep, sadly grateful that he was not and never had been, nor ever would be, its center.